TAINTED IDENTITY

CANDICE Y. DOTSON

TAINTED IDENTITY

ISBN: 978-0-578-59788-1

Printed in the United States of America

Acknowledgments

I dedicate this book to God, my husband, children, family and friends. To the readers of this book may these words fill you with love and understanding that is needed in the world today. Thank you.

TABLE OF CONTENTS

PROLOGUE

"NO!!!!!" I yelled after escaping to that usual bathroom that has the most disturbing memories a child can ever remember. For as long as I could remember this monster has haunted my thoughts ever since the first day, he made me perform an act that no seven-year-old should ever experience.

"Unlock this door…I know you hear me…. Now girl!" my mother's boyfriend yelled. His name was Darryl. He was a skinny light-skinned man that wasn't too easy on the eyes, low cut and always had this devious grin when mom wasn't looking. Who knows why he was there each day but, again my nightmare began, right on schedule? He charged in with his brown belt in hand, [SMACK] he barely missed my eye this time. "Please, please I don't want to", I cried as I slowly went on my knees. [SMACK] "Shut, up!!, he yelled, put it in your mouth" [SMACK] I prepared mentally to be somewhere else, as I did other times, as he entered my mouth.

I didn't quite understand why was this happening to me, what had I done? The evil that went in and out my mouth was viewed as the most disgusting and vile thing I have ever known. The only thoughts I had to try to sustain from the beating I would receive *"how to get out of the grip on my head" "I'm not here, I'm not here" …" when will it be over" "I gotta throw up"*

And sure enough, vomit was everywhere. "Now look what you did…. dammit?"

A sense of relief came over me as I not only spit out the disgust that just happened but also that I saw that he was somewhat at odds with what to do. I took off feeling freedom like no other, out of the bathroom and went to another apartment that was always open and abandoned. Not sure why the apartment was always empty but some of the kids in the apartment complex use it for hide-and-go-seek.

"HEY!!…. get back here!" frustration in his voice

I ran as far as I could outside. I trapped myself in the empty apartment with the cardboard boxes my best friend and I usually hide and have never gotten caught. My safe space. Still, in fear that he will find me, I re-lived each time in my mind repeatedly. My trembles were as if I was meeting God for the first time. "Serve the LORD with **fear** and celebrate his rule with **trembling**"

"Was this right to do, what did I do, what did I do?" I prayed to the Lord. So many thoughts raced through my head at such a tender age. I knew my life seemed off balance but not this. I prayed over and over until there I lay silently, motionless on the floor.

Awaken by my mother's yelling, "Well, where the hell *were* you? My child just out there by herself, if Leah didn't help me, I wouldn't have found her."

Leah was my best friend, a what they call here in the south "a high yella creole woman" in a six-year old's body standing at 3 feet 5 inches tall and 50lbs of beauty that almost blinded me when Leah yelled, "He did it!" Maybe

Leah can be the escape I need from my mom's boyfriend, but I was scared to tell her about what was going on. I didn't want her to think I was dumb enough to get myself in this type of situation. I looked up to Leah. She always gave me the courage to be strong and never put me down. But I know if I did tell Leah my mother would believe her and maybe my mother would get rid of this fungus and it'll just be me and her like it used to be.

"Wha chu talkin' bout gul, get out of he're sha?" he replied

My mom glanced at me and then asked Leah, "Did wut, girl?"

Leah's expression said it all. She knew what was up. It was practically painted on her face. I never told her exactly, but God works in mysterious ways. "I'm not sure but, I know something aint right." "This little fast gal, send her back to her mamas before they start worrying about her." He diverted.

"Well, thank you anyway, Leah…go on home, I'll talk to you later", my mom suspiciously said walking Leah to the door.

I was left alone in the room with him for 1 second too long when he mouthed the words ***you betta not say Nuthin'***"

"Alright, get out of here so I can get my baby ready for bed," she said as she entered back into the room

"Aiight, you cooked cause I'm hungry?" he responded. Mom just closed the door.

She started getting my pajamas ready and running a bath, cleaning the room as if she is getting ready to have the Lord himself stop by. After I sat there and watched her which seemed an eternity, she walked over to the bed and gently touched my shoulder. Faking as if I was sleep, I arose, and she sat next to me. Mommy was a beautiful brown skin woman with a face and smile that would remove any burden you may have. Her hair was long and black, today she has it straight but most days its curly-kinky. "How you feelin sweetie?" she asked while rubbing my head.

I wanted to scream to her what was happening,

I wanted to tell her, but I was afraid she would be mad at me.

The many times he told me 'it was my fault this was happening

I thought I did something.

I thought I was always an obedient child and all,

yes, ma'am and no, ma'am...

so how is this my fault?

Chapter 1 [DENISE]

Fear can be conquered. *"The LORD is my light and my salvation— whom shall, I fear? The LORD is the stronghold of my life— of whom shall I be afraid?"* I hope that is true or it seems to be. It's been almost four weeks since Darryl has tried to attack me. It was such a relief to find out that Mom will be staying home more now so I figured that's why no attacks. Today will be the day I tell Leah what is really going on. She has been pushing me to talk to her about how I ended up in our hideout in the middle of the night. She's pushy like that, always protective of me. As a matter of fact, that's how we met. The playground can be gruesome for a new kid and coming up I have had many days going home with River of Jordan tears.

"girl who said you can sit next to us?" said this girl who I recognized from my class but did not know her name. She seemed desperate to create an illusion in her own head that she was better than you, you and you. Self-Hate at its best.

"I don't need permission…" I replied with a side-eye

"Well, this is our area…always been. since the first grade and we don't know you, so you have to move." She said with the sass that a teenage girl has but in an eight-year-old girls' body.

"I'm not goin' nowhere."

"yes, you are!"

"Whatever!!" I fanned her away with my hand to really let her know that I was not in the least worried about her mannerisms and head movements when suddenly I feel someone grab my plait and tugged, which seemed, as hard as they have ever tugged before. I found myself in the middle of the playground trying to escape the kung-Fu grip this little hussy had on me.

"Let her go, Marissa!!" someone said next thing I know I was free, and "Marissa" was on the ground from a push that seemed to come with its own gush of wind. "You're always trying to boss people around; she can sit where she wants…. Stupid!" as she walked away, I was in a state of confusion. Here is this person that took it upon themselves to stand up for me when I couldn't, just because. In the middle of kids dispersing from the "fight area," the bell rang to go back to class. As I walked back in solitude, I was so glad the Lord gave me a break by showing that he's always there in my time of need.

It's been a year since "Ms. Can't Sit with Us" almost snatched all my edges to oblivion and my bestie, Leah, has been there through my darkest days especially since we found out we lived in the same apartment complex. Today was a pretty good day, it was almost time for spring break, and I sensed tranquility of peace and relief and today was the day I will release my darkest secret to Leah. I'm not sure how she will react so I'm on guard for whichever way it happens. I just need to let someone know.

"Did you see Marissa's project today, what was she thinking?" Leah said as she skipped backwards down the sidewalk. I hate it when she did that. It gave me anxiety as if she will fall backward, flip 30 times and end up in the middle of the street.

"Stop that!" I said anxiously

"Stop What?" she teased

"Leah!!! I said in frustration. Same thing every day; the skipping. And yes, I saw it, maybe there was no one there to help her."

"Whatever, she comes to school every day like she so better than", she said out of breath and starting to walk, "then she needs to do better with her schoolwork." Leah was always brutally honest. I liked that about her, I'm more of a people pleaser and want everything to be perfect. It has become an obsession.

"People put on for show but are really empty underneath," I replied

"Well, all I know that no tickets will be sold for that project show." She said laughing hysterically and so did I. "Why were you in the hideaway spot the other night?" Leah asked. I almost choked on the air. I forgot all about revealing my inner secret to Leah and it took a toll on me in this heat. My heart started to race a little. I started to feel like everything was in slow motion. "De-De!!!!" "Ms. Michaels, Ms. Michaels!!"

I heard Leah yelling in the background and then it's a blur.

"What.... where am I?"

I thought as I tried to arise from the bed. *"Oh, no…no…no…lay back down"* My head felt like a ton of bricks had been wrapped around it. As I laid down as slowly as if I just got my hair done and don't want to mess it up before school the next day, I tried to wrap my mind on what happened. I was about to tell Leah everything, but something came over me. Like a spirit trying to be released from the body but it's being stubborn, I couldn't get the words out.

"Hey…how you feelin', you alright?" I saw my mom sitting up on the couch with a magazine in hand with a worried yet anxious face, because she can't hide her emotions from me, but covered by a smile.

"Yeah", I said groggily "what happened?"

"When you fell you hit your head pretty hard, Leah said she tried to catch you but before she knew it you were down" she sighed. "We're waiting on some tests now." "I hate these clinics…" My Mom rubbed her face in frustration but with the style and grace, she has always possessed in my eyes. I loved my mother so much but some of the men she has been with have not been great. My father, well never met him… All I remember my mom is telling me "he's never going to come sweetie; all dreams don't come true." My first "uncle" was Russell, for the most part, he was a decent guy. On the other hand, he would hit my mom. I remember playing in the courtyard of the apartments and hearing sounds from our window. I went up the stairs to check on mom and the door flew open. I saw my mother fall to the ground and as her mouth hit the edge of the step. [POW]

*"get the hell on then, "MiMi", if you are feeling like that!"
Uncle Russell said, as he looked up and saw me with a
face, I'm sure was as stunned as he was to see me there, I
looked down at my mom as she raised herself up. The
embarrassed, shameful, look on her face told me everything
I needed to know. I ran down the stairs as fast as I could to
nowhere…*

"HI! I'm Dr. Hayila, I just wanted to let you know the
results." She said while pulling a chair to sit. "She has a
mild concussion from the fall, umm all she will need is
proper nutrition, bed rest for a few days and……. she can
take children's Tylenol for any headaches but all that
should be gone in about 24hrs."

"Ok, so we can go home, she's ok?" mom asked

"Yep, you're good to go. You can pick up your discharge
papers in the front." She got up from the chair and headed
toward the door.

"Be careful sweetie." The doctor said as she left the room

"Ok ladybug let's get you out of here…. Careful……I got
cha…. Alright, comfy?" as she adjusted the belts and
footrests on the wheelchair the hospital provided.

"Yep," I replied. Mom pressed the handicap button for
wheelchairs, once the doors came open and I can hear the
rumble of people just in disgust of the healthcare facility
they have to visit.

Mom kissed the top of my head and said, "Let's roll."

Darryl wasn't at our place when we got back from the clinic. *"Thank God,"* I thought. Before we got to the door, Leah was already waiting; as expected.

"He put his thing in my mouth," I said as if I just came into the realization of the event that has been happening since I was seven. We moved here to Baton Rouge about two years ago because my mom and her boyfriend wanted to be closer and since she was practically disowned for having me out of wedlock by her family, she said why not. She's always found work but my mother's choice in men has been far from the best selection. We moved during the summer and it was the worst day of my life. I was so confused and upset that Darryl would do this. His abusive words and intimidation were too much for my mind. I never told a soul not even mom.

"You're what?" Leah asked

"I said, He pu-…"

"What yall doing in here?" barged in Darryl. He went over to the closet rambling for something. "Don't be in here messing up everything, especially you." I felt a chill down my spine as he pointed in my direction. "James and the Giant Peach…humph?!"

"Thank God he left, ugh, he's so creepy," said Leah closing the book and leaning forward. "Now, what was it you were trying to tell me?"

"Um…I…you know what…never mind." I hopelessly said

"no, no never mind…tell me," she said with so much compassion. I thought about that finger pointing at me piercing me right at the front of my head, down my spine and out the bottom of my feet. I put my hands over my face and took a deep breath.

"Denise…. tell me, you can trust me," Leah said

Holding back tears I said "He makes me get on my knees and he puts his thing in my mouth" Leah's face was frozen stiff. I couldn't tell whether she was still alive or not. She finally blinked.

"Have you told your mom?" she asked

"No, I don't want her to think I did this…. or it's my fault…. maybe she'll be mad at me…," I proclaimed.

"Why would she…. that's disgusting!" she said with a face crumpled like a pile of tissue. "if you don't tell her, I will."

"I don't think I can," I said nervously. "I keep thinking of all the bad things he said he would do to my mom, you and me if I didn't do it..."

"ME! oh no!!!" and she took off out of the room. I got up from the bed, still with a little headache but not as much. I walked by the door and cracked it. I couldn't see anything, I backed up and Leah comes in what it seemed slow motion. She grabbed the door and slammed it shut and locked it. She grabbed me with a force so hard you swear I was in an action motion picture or something. We fell on the floor and she held me real close and that's when I realized all the commotion going on in the living room.

"You MuthaFucka!!" I heard my mom say.

"Ahhh…Git off me…git off me…ahhhh…are you crazy?" There was more commotion and started to fear that my mom needed help. I broke free from Leah and saw that "Darryl" had blood on his shirt looking up at my mother who was standing over him swaying back and forth as if she was decided whether to finish him off or let him get away with the cuts he has now. "You have two choices, stay and I finish you off or you leave RIGHT NOW and never come back," "Darryl" got up slowly holding his shoulder area and limped out of the door. I gently closed the door back and went over by Leah. "Oh my God Leah, you may want to go home, go out the window. But wait a while because "Darryl" just left, or better yet stay. How will you let your mom know where you are? Our phone is off until tomorrow."

"It'll be alright, it's the weekend, she'll be out and about anyway," Leah responded. Sounds like Leah's mother had relapsed again. I hear around the way the grown people say that Leah's mom is "on that stuff." I've never seen anything when I go visit but who knows. Leah doesn't talk too much about her mom. She seems to carry some resentment toward her mom but then loves her dearly. Living in Baton Rouge all her life she said she felt simply "trapped."

"Well, ok but stay in here, alright?"

"Alright, alright." Leah impatiently shewing me.

I opened the door slowly and took two to three steps in the living room area. I looked around and didn't see anyone there. The front door was still open. I tiptoed over and closed the apartment door. I turned to my left and seen my mom sitting on the floor with her elbow on her knees and head leaned on her wrist still holding the knife. She looked like she was talking to herself or praying. I stood in the passway from the living room and the kitchen just waiting on a moment to say something to her. I slid down on the floor to sit and simply said: "It's not your fault." She looked up at my eyes so red and puffy it appeared to be in 3D.

"What?" she asked

"I said it's not your fault."

"You could have told me, I Love you!" I know my mom would have done anything for me, but I was ashamed, abused, used, confused, pained. I got up and walked over to my mom. I took the knife from her and she looked up at me. "I'm so, so sorry that happened to you." I knelt and put my arms around my mother and hugged her like it was the last time I would ever see her again. "I'm sorry to mom," I replied. We both cried.

Chapter 2 [LEAH]

"WOW!! Leah, oh my God, where have you been? I've been trying to find you everywhere." Denise came running toward me outside of the junior high school we both ended up going to.

I haven't seen Denise since I was picked up by CPS again due to my mom's ghosting spells. It happened during the summer of our fourth-grade year. I remember it perfectly it was the time Denise told me about what 'ole boy did to her. After staying in that back room for as long as I could I snuck out of the bedroom window. I ran to my side of the complex and up the stairs to our door and went inside. As I came around toward the kitchen, *"Mom?" there he was getting doctored on by my mother. "Darryl."*

"Oh, hey baby, don't mind this go get cleaned up." My mother instructed while still tending to the most hideous human being alive, in my eyes. "How you get stabbed like this? You may need to go to a hospital?" mom suggested.

"No, I'm good…too many questions asked at ERs" he replied. I walked toward my room with my eyes grilling him up and down. He didn't see it was me due to his "demise" but hopefully, he's gone by morning.

"I'm glad she stabbed you," I thought.

The next morning, I tiptoed toward my door to see if "Darryl" was still out there. I opened the door slowly and gently trying not to make any noises. I was able to walk out to the living room and did not see anyone. I walked toward the kitchen and nothing. When I turned, I think I farted a little because "Darryl" was standing right behind me looking down with that creepy grin.

"Who you lookin' for?" he asked in a slick jokingly way.

"My mother, where is she?" I replied. I needed to see her now.

"she's not in there, she left this morning. Early. Hasn't been back and I'm ready to go. You're not my responsibility ya know." He went back into the room and plopped on the bed. "I know she got one more hour and yo a$% is going to CPS. You need to be there anyway; God knows your mama aint doing what she supposed to do for ya!" The nerve he had to talk about how someone else treats children.

"well if I had a choice between you and my mom, I'll pick my mom any day. She'll hurt herself before me unlike you" He sat up in the bed like Lazarus raised from the dead.

"What did you say to me"? he snapped

"Jes-!" I ran back into my room and locked the door. I even put a chair under it like in the movies. I sat on the floor at the foot of the bed watching the door. He never came in, but I was still on alert.

I woke up from a nap that seemed like an eternity. Someone was knocking on the door. I took my time getting to the door. "Who is it?" I asked. I DID NOT trust "Darryl" or even know how he knew my mom.

"Hi, my name is Miss Shannon Ford, I am here to check up on you since your mom hasn't been back since yesterday morning, is it ok if I come in just to make sure you're not harmed in any way?" I thought about it for a moment "regardless if she's lying or not one hand could at least be I get to have another female adult around while mom is gone, and I'll be safe from "Darryl."

I opened the door and there stood a lady with a sweet smile and hair in a bun. Her skirt was below the knee and a blouse to match. She had an hourglass figure and "Darryl" was salivating over her. "See, she's ok. It's just that I don't know where her mother is or if she's coming back or not. I'm not this child's dad and…and I want her…to.to…be in good hands ya know." "Darryl" telling the caseworker the "situation."

"Uh, yeah thanks but is it ok if I talk to her alone for a moment please?" asked miss Shannon.

"oh yeah sure, no problem…go right ahead," "Darryl" was looking like he was sweating bullets. Miss Shannon came into the room with me, shut the door and sat down on the bed. I saw a cop in the living room before she closed the door, so maybe that explains "Darryl's" nervousness.

"And what is your name dear?" asked miss Shannon

"Leah"

"Leah, what dear?"

"Anders."

"Ok, would you like to sit?" she said as she motions to the bed she was sitting on. I walked over slowly to the bed and sat a few inches away from Miss Shannon. I didn't quite trust her yet or anybody for that matter.

"So, Leah Anders, when was the last time you saw your mother?" she asked

"I'm not sure exactly, but it was the daytime," being cautious and unsure.

"So that would be at least 24hrs, how do you know Mr. Johnson?"

"Who is Mr. Johnson?"

"The man that was looking after you, Darryl Johnson." She said with a confused look on her face. I never knew his name or WAS that his real name. I've only known him by "Darryl."

"I...I never knew his name; we only call him "Darryl," I said

"Who is we?", Miss Shannon asked.

"My...I mean we as in... uh...how he plays with the kids in the apartments," I lied. I didn't want the caseworker going over to De-De's house asking questions. This is not my first time going into foster care, so I know the routine.

"Ok, I understand." She said with a skeptical laugh. "Well, honey...since we can't find your mother I will have to take to a place where you can be supervised by someone who takes care of kids."

"Yeah, I know. I much rather be there than with him. Oh, I mean Mr. Johnson."

"You've done this before?"

I nodded.

"Ok!" she stood up. "Let's pack you some items and then we can be on our way, shall we?" she held her hand out. I got off the bed and looked around for the usual items; clothes, underwear, toothbrush/toothpaste. I packed my bag, grabbed Miss Shannon's hand and walked through the door. I saw Mr. Johnson outside smoking a cigarette. He looked back at me while I waited for Miss Shannon to finish giving the officer an update. But I gave him the cold side, no eye contact, just to let him know I'm not the least bit faded at the façade he tried to put on like he cared so much. The only reason he called CPS was to get back at me for ratting him out about his little secret to "De-De's" mom. [background] "ok thank you so much, sir"

"C'mon Leah, let's go." That's the last time I had seen that apartment or my mom.

"Oh My God Heeeeyyy!!!" I yelled running toward Denise as well. I grabbed her so tight I thought I was going to suffocate her. She was my best friend and it has been a long three years not knowing where she was and if she was alright.

[SCREAMS OF ENDEARMENT SHARED]

"Where you live?" Denise asked out of breath

"You see that red 2 story house over there across the street?" I replied

"Yeah, Yeah." She was still breathing hard from her sprint.

"I live right there." I went on to give her a short narrative of what had happened with my mom, Mr. Johnson and me going into foster care. I told her I'll tell her about that place later. "Then I got adopted and now I'm here at Northeastern Middle School, Viola!" I said sarcastically.

"Wow, Leah we have sooooooo much to catch up on. Can you see if you can come over this weekend? You already know my mom is cool with it."

"STOP IT JAMES!!!" we both shouted. James Deitrick the "bully" of the school and an all-around buffoon. He decided to run right through our conversation knocking my book out my hand "accidentally" again. "Grow up James, really."

"Oh hush, girl it was an accident." He said in his usual nonchalant tone.

"Accident my behind, you get pleasure out of terrorizing people." Checking him was overdue. "And somebody is gonna surprise you onc day and turn the table, it's called Karma." Now I was in his face. He then just gave me this strange look as if he went to another place. James was dark skin, maybe about 3 inches taller than me, jet black hair and now being this close to him some of the most soul-piercing eyes that I have ever seen. It looks as if he knew everything about me without letting me know.

"Sorry, feel better now?" he said snarky as he handed me my book.

"Ugh, just…move!" frustrated I snatched my book. "C'mon "De-De" let's get to class." I took out a pen and a piece of notebook paper and gave Denise my phone number. "Here is my number. Have your mom call my mom and then we can go from there."

"Bet!" Denise took the number and put it in her back pocket.

"Ok, see ya later."

"Later." We gave each other a hug before departing to our classes. We had about one-minute left before the tardy bell rings. I went to class feeling ecstatic. I got my best friend back right around the corner and, I need to know what that was all about with James. He's never acted in such a way that was even remotely kind. Who knows and who cares? My best friend is back. Today turned out to be a good day after all.

Chapter 3 [LEAH]

It was Friday after school when Denise's Mom finally called the house. I was beginning to worry. It has only been 2 days. My mom said no sleepovers until she gets to know Denise and her mother a little better, but we can hang out in the neighborhood within our boundaries.

"Oh yes, she's been jumping for joy for a few days now. Tomorrow? Yeah, that's fine. No problem. I believe its walking distance so they can meet at the playground. Yeah…Yeah. Right, right. Ok, then dear talk to you later. Bye." Mom hung up the phone and turned around surprised to see me there but not. "Well I guess you heard everything?" she asked rhetorically.

"Sure did." as I hopped on the kitchen island bench. Most of my conversations with my adopted mom were in the kitchen. I loved to watch her cook and help when she would let me. "Ma" also known as Irene Moses was an older woman, older than Denise's mother. I would say she was in her early to mid-fifties, high cheekbones with a little meat on her bones. I remember when they brought me here, about three years ago as a foster child, she had a pleasant face and she made me feel safe.

"It'll be alright Leah, she's a good foster mother, you will get along fine." Miss Shannon said as she rang the doorbell. "Hello, how are you, Ms. Moses?" There she was smiling so bright, I almost forgot about the day I had. We walked into one of the nicest houses I have ever been in. It

wasn't a mansion but compared to where I was coming from it sure felt like it.

"Well hello there. Yall come on in" stepping aside and welcoming us in. "Alright." "Did you have any trouble finding the place?" she asked.

"Oh no ma'am, the directions brought us right here." Miss Shannon replied.

"Good, Good." "Well, who do we have here?" Ms. Moses looking toward me.

"Ms. Moses this is Leah Anders, you want to say hi Leah?" Ms. Shannon asked. I was hesitant at first but eventually came around to settling down. I always get nervous about going to foster homes. This was my third or fourth one I believe and this one seemed to have the atmosphere of being a permanent home. It's just a feeling you get when you've been moved around from different homes as I. This is what love must feel like.

"Hello," I replied.

"Don't worry honey you're safe here. I've had children come and go just like you. The Lord is with you." Ms. Moses said. I looked up at Ms. Shannon and she just smiled. So, I was a little more relieved. "Are you hungry honey?" I felt like I nodded so hard I got whiplash. "Oh ok, she laughed, let's go into the kitchen."

We walked into the kitchen and there was food cooking. It smelled good and I haven't been eating hardly anything for the past 7 days in the group home waiting while they find me a home. I hate group home food. The "box spring bed I was on" dug holes in my back, side, hip; it was like sleeping on a bed made of just sticks and stones. It would be nice to sleep in an actual bed for at least one night if this doesn't work out somehow. "This is just some tortilla soup, would you like some?" I nodded. "Ok, I need to hear that beautiful voice, I see your neck works." She teased.

"Yes please," I said smiling

"Now, that's better!" she poured some of the soup in a bowl and placed it on top of the plate she added chips on the side. She handed me the soup and gestured toward the table. "Go ahead have a seat." I walked slowly over to the table making sure I don't spill not one drop of this soup. "Would you like some dear?" She asked.

"Oh, No thank you, Ms. Moses. I think it's time that I head on out. I have one more child to pick up." Miss Shannon replied.

"Oh, bless your heart, you be careful out there." They both walked back toward the living room. I was alone in the kitchen. I looked around trying to observe more of the atmosphere I was in. "Am I safe?" I thought. It seemed to be a new home. a lot a room or maybe compared to what I'm used to. I wasn't sure if there were other kids here. I'm usually in a home with other kids. "How's the soup?" Ms. Moses asked. I was startled upon her approach being lost in my own thoughts.

"Oh, good it's really good.... Thank You." I replied

"Your welcome. I want you to know whatever you need Leah or if you want to talk feel free. I won't bite." She came and sat at the table. "Do you know why you're here honey?"

"Kind of, my mom didn't come back again," I said embarrassed.

"ok, well let's not worry about that right now. Let's finish your food and then we have to get cleaned up for church."

"Church?"

"Yes, you'll see. Eat your food." She started stirring around the kitchen tidying up.

"I think it'll be best if I didn't go back to my Mom," I thought.

****

"So what time are you leaving the house?" I asked. I was waiting for "DeDe" to hurry up with her homework. Denise said her mom is very strict with her homework, so she was breathing down her neck.

"Give me 20 minutes, I'll meet you in front of the school."

"Ok, hurry up." I hung up.

I gave Ma a kiss and left to meet "DeDe" at the park in front of the school. I didn't cross the street to the parking area because there was a gang of boys on the basketball court. I found a bench and sat to wait on Denise. "Hey," he said. There James stood next to the bench. Even though he can be an obnoxious bully, there was this side of him that seems to be begging to come out or am I the only one that can see it.

"Hey," I replied as if I wondered why he was here.

"Waiting on somebody?" he asked

"Yeah, Denise. She's late."

"Oh Ok." He said with a confused look on his face.

"What?"

"Nothing…. well…I wanted to….to apologize for the other day. I know I can be a jerk. I'm sorry." He said with so much sincerity. I didn't know what to say or why he would even care to apologize, again I may add.

"You already said you were sorry."

"Yeah, Yeah I know that...I just…. wanted to make sure we were cool."

"Yeah, we're cool."

"Ok."

"ok." there was a silent, very silent pause. All the sounds from the basketball courts or other children playing at the playground didn't seem to exist. He just stared at me for quite some time.

"Hey yall, I'm here girl." Said Denise running over out of breath. "She finally let me out. I'm like good lord how many times she has to look over my homework, Geesh." "what's up with yall?"

"Nothing!" We said in unison and simultaneously.

"Ha-ha Whatever, c'mon Leah," De-De said,

"Are yall going by the courts, come by and watch me play?" James asked all the while looking at me for approval. "It's almost our turn out there."

I looked at DeDe and she shrugged her shoulders. She was just glad to be free and out of the house. "Yeah sure. We'll be there." I replied

"Alright, sit on ya later…. I mean check… see ya later." He said nervously. He walked away hitting the front of his forehead.

DeDe and I both laughed.

We sat on the bleachers that were on the basketball court that all the boys in the neighborhood and from other neighborhoods came to play ball or hang out. It was a nice breeze out and I had my notebook and pen in hand trying to channel in something to inspire a poem. DeDe was too busy being a commentator for the game. "Look, Leah, there ya boy, ha-ha." James was acting out as usual because he felt a shot wasn't fair. "James, just let it go," DeDe yelled out.

"He's not my 'boy'," I advised DeDe. "James has anger issues. I could never see myself with someone like that. I got enough of that living with my biological mom."

"Well…ok then ha-ha sensitive are we." She teased

I sighed. "No…I was just saying. Stop analyzing everything I say." I started to write.

"I'm not analyzing you; I know you. And I know there is something with you two." She said with confidence. "it's a crush, no big deal." She assured.

"What you know about crushes and boys?" I teased.

"I know a little something. You know after you left, we found out that "Darryl" had been picked up by the police. Well, that was a relief to me, and I was able to get thru it. My mom signed me up for counseling for sexually abused kids and through the process I got better at talking more to people and being in an okay space. My head was messed up after all that had happened, so I am so glad that I went to the counseling. I'm still triggered every now and again, but I know how to cope with them. I'm not sure if I'm ready to talk to boys yet but I do know when two people are crushing on each other." DeDe said smiling. We giggled together. Denise, to go through what she had endured, it's amazing how she still has a smile on her face.

"I'm not sure if it's a crush or not but ever since I went off on him that day his whole energy has changed around me." It was an energy of some sort alright because I never really took the time to really look at James. I just noticed today that he has green eyes. Tall, dark skin but real skinny. All I know about James is that his parents split before I moved over here when he was about eight years old and he's been in this obnoxious persona since then. I felt sorry for him. I have little experience in dysfunctional households, but his behavior was not acceptable.

"Yeah, I noticed ha," Denise replied. "That would be something hahaha."

"What's so funny?" I asked confused.

"You and James? That's like an ox and a donkey plowing together." She laughed.

"Oh, I see you've been listening in Bible Study?!" Denise has been going to bible study with her mom. It helps her cope. My mom and I are at our church ALL THE TIME from the first day I step foot in her house. But I like it; keeps me grounded.

"I'm jussayin'." She said nonchalantly. We sat and watched some more of the boys from the neighborhood call for next on the court. James' team had won but looks like he still wasn't pleased with the outcome. Denise and I sat and talked some more. She went on about how she and her mom ended up moving here. Denise said she started here in December right before winter break. Here it is almost spring break and I'm just seeing her. It's too many kids at this school. She said her mom didn't bring any men around after everything that happened. She doesn't think she has been out with anyone. She ended up going to night school and then finding a job at the hospital nearby. "We're renting for now with the option to buy, which mom has already said the option is to buy the house. I didn't ask any questions." Denise did a "whatever" wave. I noticed she doesn't wear her emotions on her shoulders as she did before. Everything is just rolling off her back. I'm not sure if that is a good or bad thing.

We got up from the bleachers and started heading back toward home. We chit-chatted some more and finally made it to Denise's street. I'm the next street over. In the middle of us saying our goodbyes, we hear James running to catch up.

"Dang Leah, you weren't gonna say bye, that's cold?" he said mimicking a broken heart.

"And you ran way over here to say that?" Denise asked skeptically.

"Yeah…maybe." He said to Denise. "Can I walk you home?" he asked me.

"Well, I'm gonna head down my way, call me friend. And you be careful with my friend." Denise said pointing at James. He just waved her off. She took off down her street. Since James was walking me, I stayed at the corner until she reaches her house, about four houses down.

"Sure, you can walk me home," I told James

"Good. This way, right?"

"Yeah. I'm that house right in front of the school. So, we're not far."

"Cool…soooo what are you doing the rest of the weekend?" he inquired.

"Umm, not much. I have to do some reading and I wanted to work on my writing." I showed him the notebook in my hand.

"You mind if I…?"

"No, go ahead but, be nice." He began to read what I wrote in the park of all things. I panic; on the inside.

To my reader:

"Choose your favorite sound effect

because I am so tainted, I was scared to

put my poem in the book, Continue."

"I like it," James said

"Really?"

"Yeah, it makes me feel like everything is gonna be alright." He handed me back my notebook. I was confused and didn't know what to say or feel about his critique. James was so not who I would become friend with I thought. "It sounds like you've seen something that you like for the first time, that's a warm feeling." He explained.

I smiled nervously as we finally made it to my house. "Thanks for walking me, see ya later James." I ran up the porch as fast as I could.

"Ok, yeah…see ya! James said desperately trying to have his voice beat me to my front door. I turned and gave a quick wave. I took a deep breath behind the door before going to the back of the house.

"Hey Ma, I'm home."

"Oh. ok dear." Ma was lying down in her room watching her "stories." "You had a good time?"

"Yes, ma'am it was nice," I replied

"Well, that's good. There is food in the fridge if you're hungry."

"Alright." I went upstairs.

Chapter 4 [DENISE]

In eighth grade, I decided to pick up an extracurricular activity. I wanted to do something different; something that will allow me to express myself. I asked my mom about being in the band. She agreed if it didn't cost too much. Of course, it will cost too much, everything is too much. I tried different instruments, trombone, flute, French horn; but when it came to the reed instruments it tends to fit like a glove. I decided on the clarinet. I remember seeing a man on a black and white movie that my mom was watching one Saturday morning. When he played, it was so soothing to my ears. I felt like I had been possessed by its sound. I would practice every day, and I mean every day. I'm something of a perfectionist and I'm hard on myself. I try not to be, but I just feel I must be the best me. It's not perfect until I say it's perfect.

Today we had auditions for being a member of the high school marching band next year. I was overly excited about making the band. I don't care if I'm the last pick of the clarinets I hope I get a spot. The marching bands' performance, even though I know its hard work, has always excited me. The majorettes, flag team, and drumline are an exciting sight to see.

I asked Leah to meet me after school because that is when the results are going to be up. I need the support. But she didn't show so here I am standing in this crowd of band members trying to read this list that will determine if the rest of my day will be crappy or not. I finally got to the front and I hear Leah:

' De-De'...' De-De'… wait, I'm here." Leah shouted.

I knew she wouldn't let me down. Even though lately we haven't seen each other as often as last year. Leah is in sports; basketball, volleyball, tennis you name it. So, I understand her schedule can be hectic especially on the weekends, but it'll be nice just to have my friend for longer time periods than the quick hi and bye or a "drive-by" chat.

"Oh! c'mon let see." I said pulling her toward the list. We searched for which seemed like forever but there was my name DENISE MICHAELS under "Symphonic Band". "There it is, Yes!" I made the first chair. I found my way through the crowd with Leah. She was happy as well. She gave me a big congrats and a big hug before she jetted off to volleyball practice. I ran all the way home to tell my mom.

I finally got to the house and was out of breath to the point I couldn't find my key. After struggling to open the door and taking a deep breath of the cold A/C in our home, I was greeted by my mom and a man that I don't think I've seen before but for some reason, I felt I have. "Hey, mom, what's going on?" I asked with concern. My mother has been doing so well for herself. Yes, she has gone out on dates occasionally, but it was clear she has been making a conscientious decision to make better choices. I looked at the man that was standing in our home. I really couldn't read him as to what he was feeling. It was so much emotion in his face I started to feel a little anxiety.

"Hi sweetie, how was school?" mom asked.

"It was okay, I made the band…. who's he?" bringing my mom back to the elephant in the room.

"Sit down dear so we can talk." I slid down on the recliner we had in our living room and let my backpack fall to the floor anticipating what was about to be said. My mom sat on the couch next to me while the man sat on the couch in front of me. I looked back and forth from my mom to him a few times before she started to speak. She took a deep breath. "This is Paul Bradley, your father."

My eyes moved toward him with disbelief. Why do things happen like this in my life? Today, I received the best news and now this. I can never have just a day where even if it rains the invisible umbrella would protect me from the unfair. What does he want now that I am almost 14? I'm so confused and I'm sure my face expressed exactly that.

"Hi Denise, I'm Paul. How are you?" he asked.

I didn't know what to say. I kept staring at him to see a resemblance or something. "Fine," I said with uncertainty.

"Well, dear your father," my mom interrupted, "got in contact with me and we talked and decided that…well if you would like…. that your father starts spending more time with you?"

"But I don't know him," I replied

"Yes, I know this, he knows this." I looked at my mom in a matter of fact way, she continued, "this is why spending time gives you the opportunity to know each other." She explained.

"Look, Denise, I'm not trying to make you be okay with this overnight. All I want to know if there is any way I can have at least one chance to be a part of your life as a father?" he proclaimed.

Thinking of our previous life with mom's different boyfriends in and out, I'm not too trusting of any men. Even if he says he is my father. I wouldn't know what to do having a father. What does that feel like? I see other girls at school or in stores with their fathers and I wonder how do they feel? Are their fathers respectful or inappropriate with them? Do they truly believe their fathers love them? I'm HIS daughter, what or how am I supposed to act? There are too many emotions at this point. I needed to get some air.

"Can you excuse me for a moment?" I got up off the couch and went out to the backyard and sat on the porch swing. I took several deep breaths before I got my emotions under control. I couldn't figure out was I sad, happy, angry, insecure, terrified. It was too much for my fourteen-year-old body to take. I just sat there on the swing going back and forth with my head on the back of the swing. Just as my head seems to clear as to what I was feeling was fear, the screen door opened, and "Paul" came out on the porch. I immediately sat up and looked up at him with a non-trusting look or so I thought.

"I don't expect you to trust me" he began, "I wouldn't trust me either. Your mom…well... she told me what happened…...so I understand, and that's why I'm here. I don't want you growing up thinking that's how things are." He said with a lot of concern. And I wanted to believe him but something in me just can't let go of the fear of being vulnerable and being heartbroken. "what happened to you wasn't right, I should have been there. Me and yo mama didn't get along, but we did not LIKE each other. It was some things done and said that had NOTHING to do with you but, us working out our problems created an environment for you that was not healthy, so I felt…it was best…. therefore, I left." He put his head down at this moment and never looked back up. "I wanted to come around more and that's my fault," he finally looked up, "I should have just…" he stopped and sat in the chair next to him. "We both need healing from everything, how about we do it together?" he asked.

What choice should I make? Allow him into my life or dismiss him altogether? It would be nice to know what having a father is supposed to feel like. Going for ice cream, father-daughter dances, all the things I dreamed about how it would be like if I had a father in my life. But I know that that is just fantasy, and this is reality. And, the reality is I'm not sure what I want to do. These are not the type of problems I should be facing right now. I should be worrying about that cute boy liking me or what am I going to wear to spring formal, not *this*. The pain I feel right now makes me feel it is impossible to have a relationship with my father.

Chapter 5 [LEAH]

"So, what are your plans for the summer?" James asked. It's the end of our eight-grade year and I have noticed throughout the year James has taken a new leaf and not only turned it over but flipped and slapped it. He's so much nicer to people and you can really see his growth over the past months. We've been hanging out, just as friends, talking and sharing about our experiences. It's nice to have someone to talk to from time to time; a different perspective. I usually tell Denise everything and she would probably just feel pushed aside if I told her I've made a new friend in James. She's not a jealous person but with all that we've been through, we are all we know, and she was there through it all.

"Not sure, I signed up for this summer youth center where you can volunteer and help with elementary kids who are underprivileged so to speak," I replied.

"That's cool. I can see you doing that." He said with an admiring look. I felt a little uncomfortable. To be honest, when I'm around James and I have butterflies and my palms get so sweaty I must keep rubbing them on the side of whatever outfit I'm wearing for that day. "You have that type of personality as a "protector" or "save the world" type of thing going for you."

"Save the world?" I asked looking confused.

"Yeah, you always want to help. I like that about you, you're a good person." It did feel good to hear someone say such positive things about me. My adopted mother is good at validation at home and the church members are very encouraging along with Denise, but it was different coming from James.

"I just know what it feels like to not feel safe…I guess," I replied.

"Why do you feel unsafe?"

"Well, I don't feel unsafe right now where I'm…. living…. but I have in the past."

We sat down on the bench across from the courts. Mom usually wants me home at a reasonable time after school since I walk. I like the solitude of it, being trapped in my own thoughts, ideas, speculations, conspiracies. It may sound crazy, but I've learned a lot about myself on those walks. Now, James has been joining me on those walks. He says he wanted to just make sure I made it home okay. Funny, we both must protect. Why was he not safe? "Oh, ok," He replied fair enough."

"What does that mean, I asked confused. it's the truth?"

"I'm sure it is but, I was hoping you would let me know a little bit more about you…. maybe that was too deep. Let's start with, what's your favorite color?"

"purple, duh," pointing at my headband, ring, and earrings, "I wear this ring every day even if I don't have anything purple on."

"Why is that?"

"Maybe because it's the last thing my mom ga--..." I paused for a moment. I just realized my attachment to this ring. It became a ritual and if I didn't have it on my whole day seemed to be off-balance. How can a person that is not in your life, still be present in your life? I tried to block out the thoughts of my mother. I would pray and hope that those memories can find a hidden vault in my mind and lock itself in there for all eternity.

"Your mom……?" James pushed.

I looked at James knowing he was not going to let this go until he found out what he wanted to. "It's the last thing my mom gave me James," I replied.

"I'm confused."

"My real mother, Ms. Moses adopted me," I explained to James.

I can't believe I shared that with him. I hope he doesn't look at me differently. Sometimes I feel ashamed to have been in foster homes and now adopted. I feel like I was part of a rejected kids club of some sort or it felt like I did something in my past life on the reason why there seemed to be just not enough love for me.

"Oh okay…wow. Sorry to hear that Leah. Well, if you ever need to talk about it, I'm here." he said

"Thanks, I appreciate that."

We sat and talked some more about our families. James' dad doesn't live with them anymore, but he gets to see him often. He has an older sister she usually is the only one he can really talk to. He and his mother he says are always at each other throats. If he hears "you're just like your father" one more time he says he's going to just throw up. I laughed a little about that, but I can understand his complaint. His mom seems to be taking things out on James more than his sister and it can become stressful. Maybe that is why he would bully the kids at school. Well, more obnoxious than anything. James walked me back home as usual and I must admit.

I haven't heard from Leah all summer. Which is kind of understandable since I've been spending time with my dad on the weekends and sometimes during the week on occasion as well? It's been a process. I recently found out that the reason why my mother and father split was that my father was bi-sexual. Now, I'm not sure of the politically correct way to discuss this but the only thing I know about it is that it's an abomination per the bible. It's forgivable, from what we learned in Sunday School in Galatians, I think. When he asked me, what did I think about it, *"I don't, I just continue to pray for you and try my best to love you anyway Dad not because of that but because of you not being there..."* I explained. My problems with my father are way deeper than who he sleeps with. I understand why they couldn't be together, the obvious does not need to be explained. But, why couldn't he try harder to come around? I wanted to still know what it felt like to have a constant father in my life. I couldn't imagine the confusion he had to go thru after my mom found out. While out with mom I decided to ask her how she discovered Dad's secret, then maybe I'll have a better understanding of my mom's decisions. Which has gotten better by the way.

"Mom."

"Yeah?"

"Can I…"

"humph…girl!"

"Oh, Sorry madam. MAY I ask you a personal question?" I asked as I sprinkled cookie crumbles on my ice-cream. I love when mom and I go out for ice-cream. It's some of the best times I've had with her just sitting and talking to her. That's why I can't believe it never came across about my Dad.

"That's better…Yeah," she smiled, "go ahead." She placed her chin in her palm and elbow on the table while she picked at her bowl of strawberry ice-cream. She loved when it would get a little melted before starting to eat it.

I hesitated a little and she said, "I won't get mad." Ok, here it goes…

"How did you find out about my Dad?" I asked not knowing what to expect.

My mom sighed, "Well, I dropped you off next door at the neighbors like I always do. Your father was supposed to be already on his way to work, or so I thought. I had to come back to the house because I wasn't sure if I put your extra formula inside your bag, ya know. So, I hurried back to the house hoping to just hop in and out and still be on time for work."

She paused for a moment. She looked as if she was replaying the events in her head like she was still there. "Mom, then what happened?" I asked.

"Ya know what, nothing. You don't need to know how. Just know your father is still your father and he loves you." She stated. "C'mon let's go by the park." We got up and threw our trash away and headed out the ice-cream parlor in our neighborhood. I liked the area we lived in. It was quiet and had activities that are within walking distance from the house. We finally made our way to the park and sat on the swings. We were not really swinging but just let our bodies drift back and forth to avoid the subject that was just brought up.

"Mom, I can handle it. You had to sit through my stories. Why can't you tell me yours?" I persisted.

"De-De you are only a child and you need to stay one as long as you can. I've never spoken any ill will about your father, and I don't intend on now."

"did you catch him having sex?"

"Young lady!?!" she snapped.

"MOM! I'm fourteen years old. I know what being gay or bi- means."

"Fatha help me with this child." She turned to me. "Why do you want to know De-De, it doesn't make any difference?"

"What happened between you and daddy?" I asked practically begging her at this point.

She went on to tell me about it by saying she walked in on my father in her clothes. It was her red dress she just bought she said, which made it worse. His lover was there but she didn't "see" anything. She said she asked him about it and how long. All he said was, *"I've always been like this 'Mi-Mi'."* She said she tried to make it work because of me. She wanted to have a family and all that, but she just couldn't deal with my fathers' other life. The fights got worse the more the days progressed on until my father decided to leave.

"Did he try not to…?" I didn't know how to put it in words to ask.

"Yeah, he did. That's why I struggled with being with him but, I had to realize what was best for the welfare of you and myself in order to take care of you. Now…don't get me wrong, I've had some other relationships that were not great, but I know one thing for sure is that I'm not going to be competing with a woman for another man's love and attention let alone another man."

We just sat on the swings for a minute I guess processing all that was said. I know I was. My father didn't seem like a Darryl or something. I was just curious about what happened back then. It was a lot not said on why our life had changed. I just felt I had the right to know what kind of person I was dealing with. Trusting men is not something I'd probably get used to, maybe when I'm older, but for now my guard is all the way up.

Chapter 6 [LEAH]

Volunteering for the youth center was a good experience for me. I like to stay busy, "an idle mind is Satan's territory," as Mom would say. The kids had movie days, field trips to the museum, it was a blast for them. They could be a handful, but it was rewarding as well, and I picked up on some skills that may be useful on my resume once I really start working. I want to be a famous writer. But not any writer, I want to be a New York Times Best-Selling novel writer. A poet like Phillis Wheatley and write poems and books that tell real-life stories and struggles. "On Being Brought from Africa to America" is one of my favorite poems by Ms. Wheatley. I want my work to touch people in a way that will let them know that they are not alone in their struggles and the key to overcoming is love. Isn't that the number one commandment? Love one another?

I haven't seen James and Denise that much during the summer, so I was excited to be back at school. It's our freshman year and I was excited to start the next four years of my life with two best friends. As I stepped off the bus, I felt fear, ambition, and curiosity all at once. I walked in through the double doors from the busing area into the school. As I stopped to pull out my locker assignment and schedule my bag got knocked over by this Goliath jock. He was polite about it but it's funny how James used to do this same trick.

"Oh, my bad." said 'Goliath.' As I picked up my bag and some of the stuff that fell out of it, I slowly sighed in frustration, just enough to let him know it but not enough where he may feel bad about it. He picked up my poetry composition book and handed it to me. I grabbed the book.

"Thanks," I said with a smirk. I placed it in my bag and began to walk toward my destination.

"Tsk, you have a good day too." He laughed a little and shook his head.

I gave him a backhand wave as I spotted Denise at the other end of the hall. "Denise!" I called out hoping not to sound too "hood." She turned to look down the hall at every face she spotted until she zoned in on me waving at her for her attention. Once she realized she started pacing more rapidly as if she was on a mission of some sort. I walked toward her and found my locker amid the morning high school crowd claiming the halls. *"Ok, Leah what's the number?"* I thought to myself. I had combination lockers, I can never get it right the first, second or maybe even third time. I took the combination out of my back pocket of my new high-waisted jeans. *"2--right--16--left—and—32—right, please work"* I can't believe it, it popped right open. Leah's locker is a little further down the hall but still close. I'm not sure where James is maybe he's running late.

"Hey friend, how are you?" Denise gave me this big embrace with a sly smile I know too well.

"What you up to?"

"Nothing, why?" she smirked.

"SPILL IT!"

"OK, OK, dang." She leaned her back on the locker next to mine knowing she was defeated. Denise can't "hold water" anyway.

"Well, I ran into James this summer..."

"Yeah." I gave her the side-eye. My dear friend, in addition to not being able to keep a secret, she has a big mouth.

"Aaannd, you came up."

"mmhmm."

"And he really likes you." She finally said. I gave her this look as if I was not interested in every detail she had about James. With Denise knowing me very well, that was the main reason she "ran" into James over the summer. I'm very self-conscious and the rejection from him would probably be devastating. "I went to the corner store for my mom and he was there buying some snacks or something with his friends." She began with her story.

She went on to say he asked about me and was excited when I told him we had just hung out the day before. "He said to tell you 'hey' and he missed you over the summer, but he wasn't sure how you felt about him. He said he's been trying to call you, but you never call back. He wanted to let you know that he cares and you're the only person he can be himself around oh yeah and to call him back if you can. I haven't seen you since and I had band camp, going back and forth to my Dad's…." she explained. I listened to Denise explain why she did not tell me sooner for another 5 minutes. She gets like that when she feels she has let me down. I told her I'm not the type of friend that will not allow you to have a life. I know she loves me, and I trust that. But she is such a people pleaser. I must end this.

"Denise!", I paused as I placed both my hands on her shoulders, "I get it, no need to explain." I assured her.

"Oh, I know I just wanted to let you know." She said.

Denise and I have first period together, which is perfect. We walked to our Earth Science class in anticipation to see who we will spend the beginning of 9th grade with every morning. We walked through the door Denise first then I. I scoped out the desks and who was sitting there. The desks were enough for our students, two on both sides. I pay attention to things like that. I must be comfortable in my learning environment or I will not be bringing an apple to school every day but an attitude. Suddenly, I was off the floor and being spun around. I was so shocked I almost farted. After I broke free, I turned around and there he was.

"Where you been Leah, I've been calling you. Did your Mom give you my messages?" he said breathing heavily from the vigorous hello he just displayed.

"Yeah, I, I got it but I'm sorry I meant to call you back, but I got caught up in volunteering and amongst other things." We began to walk looking for a place to sit. It just felt automatic.

"Don't worry about it, I'm just glad to see you. So, what's up, how was your summer?" he asked.

"Hey, James?" Denise said as she came and sat down. Denise sat across from me on the other side of the desk.

"Wus sup "Dee"?"

We had a few minutes more before the first bell rung. It was the first day, so everything was delayed as far as the tardy bells and such. We sat there and chit-chatted about each other's summers. Denise talked about her Dad and the reason why he left. Poor Denise she always seems to get hit upside the head with something in her life coming back to haunt her. By no fault of her own. James said he spent the summer with his Dad working in his restaurant and going to basketball camp. I have to say it was nice to see him again. I've missed our talks.

"Do any of these people look familiar to yall?" asked James.

"Nope," I said

"Not to me, well..." Denise looked around a little. "Who is that she looks familiar?" asked Denise.

"Who?" I scanned the area Denise was looking toward. I didn't recognize anyone.

"Her, the one in the red top and red headband." Denise pointed out. I looked at the girl trying to figure out why she did look familiar. James said he had never seen her before. It was on the tip of my tongue.

"That's Marissa from grade school!" Denise exclaimed. "I knew I remembered her face."

"Who is Marissa?" I asked.

"You know, you stopped her from bullying me in grade school." She said with a laugh. I completely forgot about Marissa. But I guess you never forget who bullied you.

"Are you gonna say something to her?" James asked Denise.

"Nah."

We sat through the remainder of class. Our teacher was a short Hispanic lady, she seemed straight forward and direct. The kind of person you know what to expect of them and their expectation of you was not unknown. As we exited the class Denise said a quick goodbye and raced down the hall. Her next class was outside in the shacks for history, so James and I walked to his locker. I had history as well but inside with another teacher. James's locker was near but not close to mine. He gathered his belongings as he did, I didn't realize I was staring at his every move until James tried to ask me something and had to take me out my trance. The sound of James snapping his fingers finally got my attention.

"hey, are you there?"

"oh, year. I'm sorry." I said embarrassed.

"ok, which way you are going?" he asked

"This way." I pointed to the right.

"Ok, I can walk you if you don't mind?"

"No. I don't." I said with a smile.

"Good. Let's go." We walked down the hall not saying too much. I believe we both had a few things to say or I know he really wanted to know why I didn't call him back this summer. Of course, I was correct about my assumption.

"So why?" James broke the silence.

"Why what?"

"Why didn't you call?"

To be honest, when my mom told me he called I thought my heart was going to explode. I didn't want to be that into James and come to find out we were actually "just friends." So instead of calling him back and facing it I decided to chicken out and don't call. I know it was a coward thing to do but I panicked. Well there is my character when it comes to getting close to someone, I have more issues than the law would allow.

"I don't know, I think I had it in mind to call but never got around to it." I tried to explain.

"Around to it?" James' eyebrows went up like he was just as surprised as I was once, I heard it out of my mouth. "Around to it" is not the best choice of words.

"Well James, don't make it sound so dark."

"I'm not, I just didn't know I was on a "to do" list."

"You're not." I looked at him as if I couldn't believe he felt that way "hmm, ok. It sure seems like it. Leah don't try to act like I don't know what the real reason why you didn't call. I get it. But you can be a little more honest with me about it. It's not the end of the world." It seemed as if he shut down and I didn't like it when he did, which is so hypocritical coming from me.

"ok, then. Since you want honesty," We stopped at my classroom door. "Ok, I do like you James, I was just aforesaid of you not feeling the same way. Is that wrong to feel that way?" James just stood there tight-lipped. "I'll see you after class." I walked into class leaving him standing there.

Chapter 7 [DENISE]

Even though it was the first day, it seemed to take forever for school to let out. I headed toward the band room. We have practiced every school day during football season. I'm not sure how good our team is yet, but they better be worth all this practicing. Band practice went okay. The freshman is treated like crap of course by the upper classman but I wasn't stressing any of the formalities. I'll probably do the same thing next year but not in a bad way. I stood outside the band room waiting for Mom to pick me up but little did I know, I spotted my Dad outside waiting in his car. What was this about? Mother told me she will be here or maybe he decided to come. I always think the worst when plans change with my Mom. I think I'm still scarred from the past. It'll take time to get over and trust my Mom to be responsible, but I believe she can do it.

I walked over to my Dad's car he was listening to his Earth, Wind & Fire.

"BOO!" attempting to scare my Dad. I failed. He never seems like he is phased by anything. His personality is what you would call "cool, calm and collected."

"What, you saw something scary?" he said with a laugh. He got out the car and went over to the passenger side. He opened the door for me so I can get in. My Dad was chivalric like that. Since I've met him, he has always been very respectable. Never uttered a negative word. I think that's what I liked about him. It was different from all the other experiences I've had with the opposite sex. Yes, this is my Dad but isn't he the one that is supposed to show me how I'm supposed to be treated by a man?

"Whatever you were terrified," I said jokingly as I got in the care. He got in the car and started the engine. "where's Mom, why didn't she pick me up... I mean not that I mind you coming?"

"She's at home, I just wanted to pick you up today." He said smiling. "Maybe get something to eat."

"Cool."

"So where do you want to go?"

"Hmm, I'm not sure what I have a taste for."

"Oh Lord, are you going to be one of those young ladies that'll give her man a hard time deciding what she wants to eat. Your Mom used to do that, ugh, I used to be so frustrated." He explained. I must admit that sounded weird coming from him a little bit.

We pulled up to this little Mexican restaurant. It had a "local" look but the smell coming out of it was out of this world or I was starving. I think it was a little bit of both. We walked in and were seated. The waiter was very polite but obviously my Dad comes here often.

"Hola, Amigo." My dad greeted.

"Hola Senor Pablo, good to see you, good to see you. What can I get you?" asked the waiter. He was a short Hispanic man with a full beard and black and silver hair.

"well, my daughter here probably needs more time." He said with a jester toward me with a little laugh from our previous conversation. "But I'll take the usual."

"I don't need more time; I know exactly what I want," I replied to my dad.

"And what would that be Seniorita?" the waiter asked with a smile and a gentle laugh from my dad's teasing.

"Taco Salad."

"As is?"

"As is."

"Great choice. I'll put that order in." He gathered the menus and another waiter brought out chips and salsa. Thank God, I was just about to chew three of my fingers off as an appetizer. I skipped lunch to go check out the school clubs and other activities.

"Interesting place Dad, come here often?" I asked sarcastically

"Why yes." He smiled. "As a matter of fact, this was me and your mom spot back in the day."

"Oh, okay, what did you order?" I was curious because my Dad didn't look toward the menu once.

"I get the Chicken Florentine Quesadillas, I've tried other things here and they're delicious, but I come to Café de Sol specifically for the Florentine." He replied.

"well let's see how this taco salad goes and maybe this will become my spot." We both giggled.

"Ok, here ya go, one taco salad for the lady." The waiter placed my salad in front of me. It looked so delicious I couldn't wait to dive in. My Dad thanked the waiter for our food, and we said grace. I was so hungry I could eat a racehorse and chase the jock down for dessert. I dove straight in before my dad can say "men" in Amen.

"Did you eat lunch today?" he asked. I guess my starvation was showing as I shoveled lettuce in my mouth.

"No." my answer muffled a mouth full of lettuce as I chewed. "I skipped lunch so I can see what clubs and other non-athletic activities the school had to offer.

"Ok well finish up. I told your mom I'll have you home in time for church." He replied.

"Thanks, Dad this is nice."

He tilted his head and his dark eyebrows came together they almost look like they were stuck together. "Your welcome sweetie."

The waiter approaches our table a couple of times and the last time my Dad asked for the check. "Can you bring a to-go box senior?" my dad asked the waiter.

"Sure, Sure no problem." He replied while taking items off the table.

"And the check too."

"No problemo."

Chapter 8 [LEAH]

"Run Leah, run baby!" my mom shouted. I ran as fast and as hard as my little 6-year-old legs could go. You see, for the thousand times, my mom and her then-boyfriend was fighting. The rambling and things being thrown seem to come out of nowhere this time. My mom came in the room and grabbed me and ran out of the house. She put me on the ground once we got the street and told me to run.

"I got'chu BITCH." The man said. I turned to look, and he threw a gate chain toward us.

"RUN LEAH!" my mom grabbed my arm and pulled me closer to dodge the chain that was directly one inch from hitting the back of my heel. Once I saw the chain on the ground I looked up and the man had come by the gate and was coming down the sidewalk. He seemed to be coming closer faster than usual. His eyes were red the color of crimson and his rage overpowered my existence at that moment. Fear is all I felt.

"Aaaahhhhhhhhhhhhh" I woke up breathing so hard. That memory of my mother was buried, so I thought. Sweat was dripping down the side of my face. I wiped it with the back of my forearm moving my hair out of my face as well.

"Are you okay?" my mom came in my room and cut on the light.

"Yes, mom I'm okay. Just a dream, go back to bed." I lied back down.

"You sure." she touched my head.

"Yes."

"Okay, then I'll check on you later."

I laid there with my eyes closed having thoughts of my biological mother. I try to block them out but sometimes they appear out of nowhere. I looked at the time. "3:45 am." I took a deep sigh. I had to be up in the morning for school in two hours and now I can't stop re-thinking about what I just dreamed about. I often have these nightmares about my past life. I couldn't get back to sleep. I got up out of the bed and turned on my desk light. I looked for my composition book that I write my poems and thoughts in. It's a release that I do after each dream whether good or bad. I've tried to reread some of them, but it gets to be too much, so I try to just write them and move on. Here are the thoughts that came to mind:

"To my reader here is another poem I edited out. Keep me lifted in prayer. Continue."

Wondering where my mother is has been on my mind a lot lately. I had this same nightmare problem while in the foster homes but didn't have a release of some sort until I received counseling after being adopted. Living with my mother has given me some awful days and no hope that the future will be better. I have lived in three foster homes in which one of them I stayed because of my adoption. Ms. Moses was a foster mother at first but decided to adopt me instead. She was the most stable I had been in a long time. I was relieved that God decided to do this for me in my life, but I was worried that it was not alright to feel that way. Everything happens for a reason, I guess.

The first foster home I was in I was four years old. The lady was nice. She put me on the cutest red pants and a shirt to match with stars and ruffles of different colors. I looked like Rainbow Bright. I played outside in one of those car toys. It was yellow on the top and red on the bottom and you had to do "The Flintstone" feet to move it. I had fun. It was the most I had in a while. Next thing I know I was back with my mom. I'm not sure the reason why I had to be placed but when I got back everything seemed better at home.

The next foster home was horrifying. This was the home where there was an elderly lady and her grandson I believe. There were two other foster kids already there and we all stayed in one room. We could not go in the refrigerator. But we did eat pretty good there considering. We were allowed outside to play almost every day. There was a pecan tree, a fig tree and I believe a peach tree in the back yard. We would pick from the trees and eat the peaches if they looked ripe enough and the pecans would fall. When we got thirsty, we would just drink from the fire hose outback.

We went to church, but they didn't have any instruments or nothing it was quite boring compared to the church Ms. Moses and I got to. The church with no LIFE would teach that having music or instruments was a sin against God. But Ms. Moses showed me in the bible that we should be praising the Lord with everything we have including instruments.

It was basic living, which was okay, but her grandson was a problem for us all. He was a demon in the flesh. His name was Darrius, a weird, slightly slow fella. I'm not sure how old Darrius was but he was a despicable, perverted bag of flesh if you ask me. He would abuse the children that were in the foster home. One girl said he touched her inappropriately one time when me and the other girl Tanya went outside, and she was left in the house to clean. He would always hit us, me in particular. I remember one day I had to be rushed to the hospital because of a gash in my head by his hand.

We, as in Tanya, Clara and I, were sitting at the table eating. Darrius was in the den with us terrorizing us for no reason. He asked me something and I just looked his way to the left and rolled my eyes. The next thing I know he hit me at the top of my head with the bottom of a cup. When he did it, I didn't really feel too much pain, but I did feel kind of dizzy. But it was all the same from the other countless blows we have all taken. I started to feel something crawling down my back, or so I thought. I reached to the back of my neck to grab it and see but it wasn't something crawling, it was blood. I panicked!

"ahhh!" I yelled. I fell to the floor and started to crawl toward the kitchen yelling. "Madea, Madea!"

Madea came walking briskly toward me asking, "What's wrong?" she looked and saw me on the ground. "Oh My God! What happened Darrius?"

I didn't see him this whole time next to me. "I don't know. She just started screaming for no reason, right?" he gestured to the other two girls to say 'yes' to his lie. Madea usually believes anything he tells her about accidents or one of us crying or how something else has gotten broken. But this I wasn't sure.

"This girl just didn't start bleeding from the top of her head for no reason." She proclaimed. "Tell the truth!"

As she helped me up, I said, "He hit me on the top of my head with that green cup!"

"Darrius what's wrong with you?" she screamed.

"Wha-, I--- I--." He stammered his words, I guess because of the way Madea yelled at him.

"Just get some towels and meet us at the car Boy!" while Darrius went to get towels, we all walked outside to the carport where the car was. Darrius came running out a little later. Madea snatched one of the towels from him. *"what took you so long?!"* She placed the towel on the seat of the car, so my head won't get blood on it and placed another towel on my head and told me to press hard. She got in the car and closed the door so hard I thought the window was going to bust. Darrius was standing outside looking dumbfounded. She yelled out the window, *"Try not to get into any more trouble, can ya do that?"* We pulled out the driveway and headed toward the hospital.

We walked into the hospital. I was starting to feel a little dizzy. Madea sat us down and went to the counter. I started to close my eyes and the next thing I know Madea is taking my arm and guiding me down a hall to a room. The room had a bed a chair and other wires and stuff that I didn't know anything about.

"Get in dear." The nurse said. I got in the bed and laid back. *"Just relax, the doctor will be in soon to check you out."* She had temporarily wrapped my head to slow the bleeding. The nurse left the room to get the doctor I suppose, and I was there with Madea and the two other girls in the foster home with me.

"Now how did this happen?" Madea asked Tanya, I guess since she was the oldest of us.

"Exactly how Leah said, he hit her with the cup. He's always hitting us." Tanya revealed.

We all looked at her in astonishment. Clara and I looked because we were threatened so much not to snitch or tell, I would have never thought Tanya would have said anything.

Madea was just stunned because the perfect image she had of her oh so beloved grandson was shattered into little pieces in a matter of seconds with a few words.

"Well hello, I'm Dr. Hill. Now what's going on here?" He took the bandages off and looked at my wound. "Hmm, okay. It looks like she will need some stitches not that many, but I want to run some tests just to make sure everything else is okay. Sounds good?" he looks at Madea.

"Oh Yes, yes doctor no problem. Thank you." Madea replied. The doctor left out the room and soon after these two nurses came to take me for my stitches and test. I heard the doctor call Madea over to talk to this lady in a business-like suit. "Yes, I'm here." She walked over to where the lady and doctor were standing as I was being pushed down the hall.

I was sleeping the whole time they put in my stitches and put me in the MRI tube. When I woke up, I was back in the room, but it was me and the lady in the business suit. Madea, Clara, and Tanya were nowhere to be found.

"Who are you?" I asked the lady

She turned her head from the T.V. on the wall and smiled. She stood up and walked toward me and sat in the chair next to the bed. "Hi Leah, my name is Shannon Ford. I'm your caseworker. How are you feeling?"

"Okay, I guess. Am I going back to...?" I started to ask but she saved me the time.

"No, never." She said. "Your mother has gotten herself together Leah so you will be placed back with her. We will make visits and check in on you and her from time to time to make sure everything is alright. How does that sound?" 'How does it

sound'? it's a whole lot better than what I just came from lady. Now that I look at this Miss Shannon, she does look familiar. She has been my caseworker from the last time I had to go to a foster home.

"That sounds fine, I miss my mom anyway," I replied.

"Good, let me go get the doctor and let them know you are finally up. They probably give you another look over then we can get you discharged and back home. I'll be right back." She smiled and walked out of the room.

I sat there thinking about the events that just occurred and why were they happening to me. I'm on my way to be united with my mother and hopefully, this is the last time. But I had to get my head busted in? Why can't things just go more smoothly? Has God forsaken me or are these just the woes I must endure? I just wish that my life can be stable without so much turmoil. I'm too young to be weary.

"Okay dear let's look you over one last time and get you out of here safe and sound." Dr. Hill said as he lifted my head gently.

That day was the end and start of a new life again with my mother or so I thought. I had hoped it was the last time I'll be transitioning from another home, but it wasn't. Sometimes I just felt like I needed another mother. I love my mother, I really do. And it seems wrong that I would feel this way, but it is reality.

Chapter 9 [LEAH]

I remember the day I met the guy I knew was the ONE. At this point in my life, I'm about fifteen and really growing into myself. My mother saw me off to school that day which was weird because she's usually gone being a morning nurse and all.

"Be careful out there 'sweets' see ya later," Mom yelled from the front door.

"Alright, bye!" I yelled back running down the street to catch the bus that passes my house. I hated the fact it couldn't just stop in front of the house. I live at the halfway point between the two stops on the street. I got to the bus stop just in time. I think the driver slows down a little to give me time to catch up. That's the least he could in my opinion. The bus pulled up and I got on and sat in my assigned seat.

The bus ride was the usual. Kids loud mouthing each other, the neighborhood bully in the back of the bus and the fifteen-year-old wanna be playa trying to smooth talk you. Today I wasn't having it. The hand immediately went up when Ty slid into the seat next to me, thank God we were almost at the school so it would be on two minutes to endure of his begging. "Nope, not today Ty."

"Dang, girl every time I--." He started. I placed my hand up again.

"What did I say?" with a smooth side-eye and hand gesture Ty began to back off. To also add we were pulling up to the school.

"Alright, alright you win this time Leah, one day," he looked at me up and down like a wolf hunting sheep. I wonder who was the chick that gave him some already. Take a cold shower, will you? "...for real one day." He continued and walked back to his seat with a sly grin on his stupid face.

I got off the bus and entered Phillis Wheatley High School once again for my sophomore year. Unfortunately, Denise got rezoned and ended up at another school, but we still see each other on the weekends when we can. James is still here but he's so into playing sports I see Denise more than I see him. James and I decided to stay friends since it seemed too complicated for me. I just felt James wanted to get closer because he hasn't had anyone that really cared about what he thinks for a change.

Later, that morning after the first day formalities, I walked into my 2nd-period class. I sat in the middle far right of the class. I wasn't aware of who was in the class yet. I was just in the middle of getting settled in when this fool tapped the leg of my desk with his foot and said.

"Uh, Good morning?!" he said. I turned to my right and saw the most gorgeous thing in the world. He was of almond complexion with the most mysterious grey eyes and a smile that would blind the sun. I played it cool hoping that what I'm really feeling is not showing all over my face.

"Uh excuse me, that is no way to greet someone. Try again!" I said rhetorically with an eye roll. The eye roll was just to hide the gloss that was layered over my eyeballs after the view I just had.

"Well, the next time you come in you say 'good morning' I know you were taught that. You look like the type that was taught that." He had this sweet smile on his face with each word that came out of his mouth.

"Donnie, leave her alone and face the font." Said Ms. Wilson our Math teacher. I giggled a little under my breath. I thought *'Donnie? I wouldn't have thought of that name for him but whatever.'* Ms. Wilson continued. "Leah, don't let Donnie get you in trouble." I gave Donnie the side-eye and of course he was looking right at me with that little smirk.

Over the course of a month or so I learned a lot about Donnie. Something inside me just caught on fire when I would see him. I think it's because in getting to know him was like understanding myself more. We had a lot in common. I remember the first time he tried to ask me out. Ms. Wilson had come up with an idea to have partners in class. Of course, Donnie moved his chair so close to me as fast as he could. The guys behind him teased but he didn't care. Jocks!

"Yeah, yeah whatever. Mind yall business." He said to the guys he knew sitting behind us. "What's up Leah?" he said smiling.

"Hey, Donnie," I said with the biggest smile on my face completing the last problem we just went over. "You couldn't team up with no one else?"

"Nope. Why would I?"

I shook my head. "Let's start with the first Unit and go back and add to the notes like we've been doing. Cool?" I'm usually partnered with Donnie. He was a nice guy and very laid back. He had a certain way about him that I was drawn to, but he needed a little help when it came to Algebra. He wasn't ashamed to say it either. As a matter of fact, he didn't seem to have any shame about anything. His jock friends would clown him almost every day, he would just smile and keep it moving. People would hackle him when he's at the blackboard and he would laugh it off. It bothered me but then I believe the lesson is that Donnie knew how to smile and blind the hate.

Donnie leaned in and in a low voice careful about no one to hear and angled himself so that Ms. Wilson couldn't see him. "Wanna go out to the movies with me?"

"What?!" surprisingly I said.

"Go out with me, ya know a date."

"I don't know, my mom is kind of strict."

"Ok, well is there some other way I can see you other than in here?" he persisted.

"I don't know", I paused a bit. "I help at the youth center on the weekends and..."

"Ok, where is that and I'll come see you?" he looked up to see where Ms. Wilson was. Today was Wednesday so I had until Friday to figure out if I'll give Donnie the address. Sometimes my mom will pop up at the center for a "visit."

"Ok, let me think about it and I'll let you know before the weekend, alright?" I asked.

"Of course." He sat back in his seat and licked his lips and just stared at me. I changed the subject to get out of my daze.

"Unit one…" I continued with the lesson.

It was Friday morning and after talking with Donnie more and finding out that my mom would be doing some volunteer work at the church, I decided to accept Donnie's invitation and provide him with the address to the center. I walked into class and sat down. I began to go through my work for the day and noticed Donnie was not in his seat yet. The bell rang and Ms. Wilson closed the door. As I looked back, I prayed that Donnie would come running through like he usually does when he's late. No Donnie. Ms. Wilson walked to the front of the room.

"Ladies and gentlemen listen up please, listen up." The room got quiet from all the pre-class chatter. "I have some unfortunate news; our dear Donnie has passed away." The room started to chatter again at a much higher volume. "Settle down please, let me finish." Ms. Wilson said to gain back control of the class. "Now I know this is some shocking news, but further details will be given later. We are just finding this information out our ourselves." She walked back over to her desk. "Let's take out your unit books."

I was in more than just shock, I was crushed. What type of God would place love so close to your reach and then snatch it away? I turned to the guys behind me. "What happened?" I asked.

The one that sat behind Donnie looked at the others before answering me. "He was in a car accident. He…. he took his dad's ride because he found out where your center was, so he decided to ride by to see if you were there but never made it." He put his head down as if he was bracing for my reaction. And he was right.

"You're lying," I accused. "You're a liar."

"Leah…" he reached out.

"NO!" I got up and walked toward the door. I can hear Ms. Wilson calling my name but I kept on walking out the door. How can he tell me that? "Donnie WHY!?" I cried. I had made my way to the girls' bathroom. I hid myself in a stall so no one can see my pain. This had to be one of the worst days of my life.

I barely made it through the day and went straight home. I tried to write my pain away but could never release it through the pen. I spent the weekend in bed or just in my room being surly or sobbing. I didn't go into the center that weekend as well. I reflected on everything I thought love was supposed to be. I should have known it wasn't going to be that easy. Should I still believe in love or should I let it die as Donnie did? That is a hard choice to make especially since love chooses you sometimes even if you try to outrun it. Well from here on out that's what I vow to do, outrun love. You won't catch me anymore just to torture me and then reel me back in for more.

Chapter 10 [LEAH]

I ended up getting a job at the local record store nearby. This was a good place for me for inspiration and an outlet from the devastation of Donnie. I liked working there listening to the newest LPs and meeting new people with different tastes and interpretations of the art. I was reorganizing and replacing LPs when the door opened because the bell rang at the top. It was James walking thru and a girl of my same height or a little taller or so, slender and melanin as deep as Mother Eves firstborn. I stood up to get a better look. Just as I thought, Marissa. Can you believe this? I walked over to the register and just watched every move they made. What was James doing with Marissa? Better yet, how did this happen?

"Oh, wus up Leah? I didn't know you worked here." James said as he and Marissa made their way toward the front of the store.

"Yea for a few months now," I replied smug like.

"What's wrong with you?" James asked.

"Oh, hey Leah, longtime no see." Interrupted Marissa right on time. She was just that type of person. Always ten steps ahead. "Sorry to hear about Donnie, I understand you two were close?"

No, she didn't. Marissa can be a sneaky, conniving little alley cat and will stop at nothing either to get what she wants or to avenge anyone she has it out for. "Always a pleasure Marissa, always. Is there anything else I can help you'll with today?" I moved my eyes back and forth from James to her.

James gave a soft "No."

"Oh, we fine," Marissa added.

"Ok, that will be $5.47." I held out my hand to receive the money from James. Marissa walked over to a stand with new releases. James reached over to place the money in my hand and grabbed it at the same time.

"Talk later?"

"Wha-!"

"Talk later!?"

I pulled my hand away and gave a suspicious nod. James gave me a look of relief that hopefully, I would agree to talk to him. But why wouldn't I? James and I have never been involved or was it some deep emotion toward Marissa from back in the day. Either way I was just ready to get them both out of there.

"Alright girl, see ya around," Marissa said as they exited the store.

The whole incident with James and Marissa bothered me. I couldn't wait to finish my shift so I can get home and call "DeDe". I didn't like asking my mom for rides. I wanted to be more independent so I would take the bus home. This night of all nights when my emotions are high, I'm late getting off and I'm here standing out in this hot southern humid weather. Standing at the bus stop contemplating whether I should go back inside and call my mom, a car pulls up. Once it had gotten closer, I saw it was a classmate of mine that I've known since grade school. Lewis Nichols and his flashy car that all the girls stick their butt out for.

"Hey Ma, you need a ride?" he offered.

I didn't know too much about Lewis other than he grew up in our same neighborhood and both his parents had decent jobs. He was a bit of a womanizer in my opinion.

"No, I'm alright," I replied

"well, you might not be, the bus just passed about 5 min ago so…" he leaned over and pushed his door open to his Oldsmobile I think it was a cutlass. Lewis was a grade ahead of me, so I was skeptical of him being nice. We did live in the same neighborhood but never really said too much to each other just a nod here and there. "Get in, I'll take you." He said trying to see me from his driver side with his light brown eyes glaring in the moonlight or it could just be the taqueria lights flashy giving me this effect.

"Ok, thanks." I got in. I mean wait another twenty minutes for mom to get here or go now. I put on my seat belt and sat as close to the passenger door as possible. Lewis was taller than me about six feet and athletic. He played football and basketball since I could remember. I still was on alert you never know how people really are.

"Relax", he laughed a little, "I'm not gonna hurt you." He said as he looked for something to play on the radio.

We pulled off from the bus stop down the street. "Casanova" by Levert was playing on the radio.

"So how long have you been working there?" Lewis asked.

"Not long."

"ok, ok." He looked my way a few times. "You know I've seen you around, Leah. You never look like you want to be bothered."

"Why would you think that?" I asked in confusion.

"I don't know, I guess the times I try to speak to you or have a conversation…just say it's not always the right time." He explained.

"I didn't know you were trying to have a "conversation" with me. What did you need to talk about?" I said in an okay I'll bite tone.

He laughed a sly laugh as to admit he's been caught, and his game blew up in his face. "To be honest, nothing. I guess I was just curious about you." He said with a smirk while we stopped at a traffic light.

I looked straight ahead as long as I could. I looked to my left and Lewis was staring right at me waiting on a response. I didn't want to give him one. All I wanted was to go home. "Well, I'm glad your curiosity has been satisfied. Once you get to the next light make a left, please."

"I know." He said. "We live in the same neighborhood, remember."

He navigated through our neighborhood with me telling him a turn or two and we finally arrived at my house. "Thanks Lewis, I appreciate it," I said as he put his car in park.

"No problem, if you need me to pick you up sometimes…. just let me know. It's no problem" He said with a smile.

I rolled my eyes a little with a smile. "Ok Lewis, thanks anyway." I got out of the car. Lewis leaned over to help close the door.

"Alright, no problem."

I walked to the front door and put the key in. I turned to see Lewis creeping slowly as he waited for my signal that he was okay to take off. I heard his Cutlass down the road as I walked in the house. Mom was sitting in the living room recliner sleep. I covered her with a blanket and headed to my room. I plopped on my bed and closed my eyes to run through my thoughts and clear my head before getting ready for bed.

"it would be nice to have a ride from work instead of the bus, but this is Lewis it would not be a smooth transaction. I'll offer gas money, yeah, I was paying the bus fee anyway. I'll run it by Lewis later after I've thought about it for a while. I just don't trust him." I looked at the clock on the wall. *"It's late, Denise probably is studying and won't take any calls or its past her time to talk. It's the weekend. I'll call her tomorrow about this Marissa and James thing. So far, I like a boy that is with someone else, the one I thought*

I could have loved died and now another shows up out of convenience. With these pickings who needs leftovers."

Chapter 11 [LEAH]

I sat at the table eating a light breakfast while on the phone with Denise. She had band practice before a parade they do every spring, so she was up early. I was up early as well because I couldn't get rested well enough to sleep a full hour because of this James mess. I told Denise about him and Marissa showing up at the store. Also, I made sure I emphasized the audacity of her mentioning Donnie to me in front of James, it being too soon and the fact she doesn't know me that well to be THAT concerned. Denise was rugged and livid at the same time about this situation. Even though I try to hide it I do like James, but he can be unclear sometimes, so I didn't want to "play" myself. Denise is the only one who knows this, so she is determined to make sure this Marissa story does not take place, a two for one for her.

"No, she didn't. Have you talked to him?" Denise asked digging in for clues on where to strike.

"No, I haven't made up my mind if I want to or not. If I do, then the conversation may drift toward me and him and you know how emotional I can get?"

"Yeah, true."

"Then if I don't, then I would never know, I guess. Right?"

"So, what you gonna do?" Denise asked. "You want me to see about it?"

"No, no." I took a deep sigh. "I'll just let the universe deal with it. I don't want to worry about it. I just want to do my writing and get through school." I decided.

"I understand that, well gotta go. If we're late we got to do laps. You're gonna be ok?" Denise asked concerned.

"Yeah, go 'head, I talk to you later. Bye girl!"

"Alright, bye!"

BUZZZZZ…

I hit the alarm a few times before my mom tapped on my door. "Ok, Leah lets go.!"

"I'm up," I said with a heavy sigh.

I was not ready for Monday morning. My weekend was uneventful despite Fridays' events with James and Lewis. All my homework was done, and I was ready for another week, but my body wasn't. I dragged myself into the bathroom to do the morning routine of picking apart my face, hair and then putting some type of cover up on. Being sixteen going on seventeen is for the birds. I feel like I'm stuck in the middle of childhood and adulthood. I finished getting ready and grabbed some toast before heading out to catch my bus. Kissed mom bye and told her I'm on the schedule to work after school. I walked out the door and was stopped in my tracks.

"Good Morning!" he said. I stood there with my mouth open as I walked slowly toward the end of the driveway.

"What are you doing here?" There he stood with that smirk on his face that shows off dimples to die for. He leaned back on his car folded his arms and crossed his legs.

"I was on my way to school so I figured I'll stop by and catch you before you caught the bus and see if you would like a ride instead."

"Do I have a choice?" I asked

He laughed. "You do but, why choose the bus?" he got up off the car and opened the door. "C'mon before we're late." I hated the overbearing way Lewis can be. He has a very determined and ambitious personality. It's either his way or the highway. Of course, I stepped into the car and gave Lewis a disapproving glance, but I'll let him slide this time. He knew it as well as he closed the door after I got in. Lewis got in and took off down the road. "I just wanted to surprise you that's all." He finally said

"You have a way of surprising someone that's for sure."

We pulled up to the street to turn into the student parking lot. There were kids out hanging out in front of their cars, smoking the whole typical teenage activity. Lewis parked away from the 'crowd.' "We're kind of early," Lewis said.

"Yeah, I usually don't get here this early, riding the bus and all," I replied.

He smiled a little and shook his head. "Leah, Leah."

"What? And why do you always do a little laugh every time I say something. It's kind of annoying?" I asked a little agitated.

"I'm annoying you, Leah. Wow!"

"I'm talking about your behavior, Lewis."

"Well okay, you know what's annoying to me?"

"I'm sure you're going to tell me." I rolled my eyes a little.

"That right there. Why must you always give me the cold shoulder? What have I done?"

I unbuckled my seatbelt and turned to face Lewis. He was sitting in the driver seat with his elbow propped on the window seal of his door and his head rested in his hand waiting on my next response as if he already knew what was going to come out my mouth. "Lewis, I honestly think you're an overbearing, overhyped, womanizing misogynist. But I shouldn't assume you have such an extensive resume before knowing for myself. So, I guess my "coldness" is me really being "cautious." No offense!" I said with both my hands up as to wave a white flag.

"You really think I'm overhyped?" he said with the brightest smile.

"Out of all the other stuff, I said, 'overhyped' is what you're concerned about, ok?"

We both laughed.

We both got out of the car and walked toward the building. I can still see that Lewis was marinating on the explanation on why I act the way I do with him even though he did it with a smile. "I admit I like the ladies and it may appear that I have no soul when it comes to the matter of the heart, LEAH…" I turned and looked at him laughing, "but I do. You'll be surprised how some of these girls do me."

"Yeah right!" I said with doubt.

"Seriously, what, you don't think dudes don't get their feelings hurt. Yall can be cold. No offense." He teased. "look how you do me, with your shortness and 'talk to the hand' persona." Lewis made a gesture as to imitate me. I must admit it was hilarious and I haven't laughed that hard since Donnie. "I'm just sayin though, what's up Leah?" I knew Lewis wanted to know me better, but I wasn't interested in dealing with anyone.

"Lewis…" I began.

"Hey, Leah?" I looked up as Lewis and I walked in the school building and there was James standing with a few of his football friends. He said my name so loud it caught me off guard.

"Oh, Hey James." I did a short wave and kept walking with Lewis. Lewis did a quick nod to James as guys do. To be honest, I had a quick panic attack seeing James. I wanted to talk to him about what happened, but I wasn't ready, but I may have to face the music. I said a quick bye and thank you to Lewis after I let him down about dating.

"That's alright Leah, you'll change your mind. I'll make sure of that." He headed down the opposite hallway.

"Later Lewis."

I ended up at my locker with who else but James waiting there with all his drama. As I put in my combination, he just stood there with a sad puppy look. "What James?" I said with a long sigh.

"You tell me. Why I haven't heard from you? And what are you doing with Lewis?

"He gave me ride I mean we do stay in the same neighborhood." I said derailing from the actual truth. "And honestly I thought you would be busy you know, with your new relationship and all." I started walking toward my class with James tagging along.

"She's not my girlfriend if that's what you're talking about, Leah." He explained

"Okay, it's your choice." Trying to blow off the fact that I was actually jealous. I was more hurt that he didn't tell me. Whether we are involved or not he's still my friend.

"Can we talk about this later, Leah?"

"No, it's fine. I'll catch you later, James." I headed toward my class leaving James in the middle of the hallway. I didn't want to talk about it anymore. I didn't want to deal with the matters of the heart and the attachments that can cause a strain on my well-being. The goal is to get through high school without falling into the trap of falling in love and having it turn into a life that I didn't dream of having. To be plain I don't want to turn into my mother and as I continue through life, I find myself running from the thought on a constant basis.

Chapter 12 [LEAH]

"Who is this guy you're going to the Jr. Prom with?" I asked Denise as I sat and watched her get ready. We were in our senior year. Graduation and prom were the most important thing in our lives at this point; well in other people's lives. I wasn't too interested in going to my senior prom. I had been asked by a few guys at school in passing but no one that I would go with.

"His name is Nathan Carter, he's a junior. I started talking to him at the beginning of this year remember?" Denise reminded me.

"Oh yeah, I remember. You don't feel funny dating a junior?"

"Why would I?" Denise looked at me with a strange face. I wasn't sure what she was really thinking but I think I struck a nerve. "He's a cool guy, respectful, really into his studies, what is there not to like?" she said defensively.

"I wasn't trying to put any doubt in your friend, I'm sure he's great." I didn't want Denise to feel uncomfortable or put her in a negative mood before the dance.

I helped Denise finish getting ready and we went into the living room. Ms. Michaels was standing with a camera in her hand and moving around things in the living room. I believe she was setting a background for the numerous pictures she was about to take. Nathan was already downstairs waiting on Denise. He was a tall Carmel skinned toned with big brown eyes. His suit fit him well. It was some thought put into it. He had a red bow tie that matched his black blazer and pantsuit with a nice embellishment design throughout the entire fit. I have to say the brother was clean. Denise lit up like it was Christmas. I never seen her so smitten you might say. Denise smitten? I'm not sure when this happened but I'm going to find out.

"Oh, Denise honey, yall come over here so I can get a couple of pictures." Ms. Michaels

"Mom don't fuss. Hey Nathan!" Denise said with this gigantic grin.

"Hey." He said with the same grin. It was almost sickening. "I brought you a corsage, I hope you like it."

Denise's' dress was red with silver embellishments from the waist up which matched Nathans' bow tie. Her accessories were silver as well. The two of them made a cute couple. To be honest, I was a bit jealous. I did wish to "have" someone but was not willing to go through the process. Like mom says, *"Sometimes you have to pay to play."* Well I'm broke so no thanks.

"Well, well, well. Let me look at you? Just beautiful like your mother." Denise's' Dad walked in from the back. I didn't know he was here.

"Of course, she didn't get it from you." Ms. Michaels teased.

We all laughed.

"Thanks, Daddy," Denise said so proudly as she embraced her daddy tightly but not so to mess up her look.

"How are you doing young man?" said Mr. Michaels

"Great, just waiting to take out the most beautiful girl in the world," Nathan responded.

LAME!

"Ha, Ha, you hear that "Mi-Mi" he is laying it on thick?"

"Leave them alone and move so I can get some pictures." Ms. Michaels replied,

"Oh hush, you've been taking pictures the whole-time woman." He said as he still moved out of the way.

"Just telling the truth," Nathan said.

I thought it was corny.

"That's right Nathan you tell 'em," I said

"Oh, I'm so sorry, Nathan this is my best friend Leah." Denise introduced me to Nathan finally, but I understand. "Nathan- Leah, Leah-Nathan."

"Nice to meet you." Nathan stretched out his hand.

"Same."

Nathan and Denise took maybe another thousand pictures before heading out. We all said our goodbyes and the cute couple hopped in Nathans Chevy El Camino, which so happens to be red and went on their way.

Truth be told I was happy for my friend. Truly. It's just that I didn't want to see Denise's' relationship and then feel the need for my own. I wanted to stay true to my commitment I set forth myself and stick to it. I had other plans and it did not involve any teenage love or any love until I've accomplished what I set out to accomplish.

Chapter 13 [DENISE]

I started working at the local grocery store about almost a year or so ago. That's where I met Nathan. He was the pretty boy type but after getting to know him a little more he wasn't what I expected. He was kind, thoughtful and a good listener. Being skeptical of past experiences I thought something was wrong with him. I asked my mom why I would be afraid of him.

"Afraid of what Denise?" mom asked

"I dunno, what if he's really not a good person or a little decent. I'm not perfect but…?" I hesitated

"But what?"

"I just feel I'll always be looking for the "Darryl" inside every man because of my past. How do you completely get over that? How do you try to move on?" I asked

"By faith, not by your sight. You're going to have to learn to live your life despite of…. of anything that may happen in your life. I know it feels like it's only the beginning for you and it's been a bit rough already but keep on living. There are going to be things that God will show you to let you know that he is with you. Always." My mom responded. "It'll be fine. Pray about it."

"I sure will mom. Thank you. I needed to hear that."

Nathan had been asking me out for almost two months now. After about a month or so he started to be more direct.

I was unaware for about a month that he really was sweet on me instead of just being nice.

"Evening," Nathan said as he passed me coming from the breakroom. He always would speak or stop me for small talk in between shifts. This time is where he got my attention.

"Oh, Hi Nathan." I waved back

"Hey, when do they have you scheduled for break?" he asked

"Umm, its usually 2 hrs. after I get here but it depends, why?"

"Do you mind if I join you, just for 5 min I swear?" He held up his hands as if that represented no deceit.

I waited for a few before I responded. Five minutes is not bad. I had what my Mom said in my head. What's wrong with five minutes? Ok, I'll bite. "Ok, yeah sure, is something wrong?"

"No, no, no. Nothing like that." He laughed a little. "I wanted to tell something, it's not bad. Well, I hope."

"OK. I'll let you know when I'm on break, ya know if I see you in time."

"Ok, Cool."

I clocked into work and got my till for my register. It wasn't that busy today. I like cashiering. It helped my social skills in dealing with people from all different walks of life. There were some heathens, but you still must love them too. My floor supervisor came over and cut my light off. I had been working for three hours so I was ready for a break anyway. I checked out my last customer and locked my register. I bought my self some water and a cheese and cracker snack. The one with the red stick. It wasn't the healthiest but hey I spent most of my money on band stuff and helping mom so this would do until I get off in another couple of hours. I went through the fast line and Nathan walked behind me.

"Oh, you're on break?"

"Well, I guess you caught me," I replied sarcastically. To be honest I wasn't going to tell him I was on break. I punked out a long time ago. I just decided I'll go on break and if I see him, I see him.

"well, I guess I have. Is that 5 minutes still up for grabs?" he asked

"sure." I replied semi-reluctantly.

After he paid for some gum, we walked outside of the store. We didn't walk that far from the front but enough where we could hold a conversation. "Gum?" Nathan offered.

"No, thanks." I waved away the gesture.

Nathan leaned on the side of the wall of the building. He looked up at me with a grin and a face to contemplate his next statement. I kind of liked that about him at times. He seemed very patient to be his age. He had an old soul. The stereotypical personality that one may think a pretty boy may have was far from who he truly was. There was a car, but it wasn't flashy to me, he did work which was good but so did I. I'm definitely not the female stereotype that's been going around lately in the '80s, the unattainable, perfect object of desirability. From what I've been through I try to stay away from being the visibility for a male protagonist. Yes, I would like to be a helpmeet as the word of God says but not at the expense of being me. Who am I? The movement of cherry blossoms in Spring on a windy day. Then the sun shines down on them as if God telling them 'Yes I see you my creation.' So, even though the most handsome young man is standing in front of me now, I will not, I will not be caught up in the sight of him.

"I've been meaning to talk to you for a while now." He said with a smile now. "But, you're always on the go. So yeah I'm glad I caught up with you." He laughed a little.

"Oh, well I was unaware I was being chased." I always took the witty approach it calms me. "So, what is it you had to tell me?"

He waited for some people to pass by before saying, "I like you, Denise. I think about you all the time."

"okay" I didn't know what else to say.

"That's it" he laughed a little nervous laugh. "I don't know what now, but I thought I would…" He paused. "I just wanted you to know." He stood up off the wall and threw his gum paper in the trash next to us. "Well let me get back, and if you want to go out to the movies or need a ride or something, just let me know. See ya later." He walked back into the store. I guess he really meant 5mins.

Nathan went to another school not too far from us but not zoned in our area. He was a sophomore and I a junior, but it didn't seem to matter. He seemed prince-like. Mature for his age. I was impressed. I went back into the store when my break was over. I saw Nathan was talking to one of his coworkers that worked with him in the stock room a little distance away, but we still managed to catch each other's eye as I opened my register. I gave a gentle smile and began to check out my customer.

My shift to go a little quicker than usual today. I checked out my last customer and removed my Till and turned it into the customer service desk. Clocked out and was headed toward the door when I noticed Nathan sitting in front in his car. I walked further out of the store and try to act like I didn't see him sitting there and just began walking toward the bus stop.

"BEEP-BEEP"

Nathan rolled down his window to his black and silver Chevy El Camino SS. I liked his car. It was vintage old, but it fit him. He told me it was his uncles' old car from 1976, I think. When he turned sixteen in July his uncle gave him this old car. It was just sitting in front of the yard. It was still in good condition. So, he told me he spent his first paycheck on a paint job and went on from there. He helped his dad at the garage sometimes to earn extra money to fix his car too. I think he wanted to show his dad he could work for what he wanted instead of it being handed to him.

The deal is Nathan was a little more well off than my family was. His Dad and uncle owned a few automotive shops around town. Nathan wasn't really into fixing cars for a living or running a business. He said his passion was really cooking but he knew his father probably would be disappointed for going that route instead of taking up the family business.

"Hey, Denise c'mon!" he gestured for me to get in.

"OH, I'll take the bus, but thank you."

"Girl, if you don't get in." he reached over to the passenger side and opened the door.

"Are you sure?" I asked for no reason at all but to stall.

Nathan gave me a 'stop it' look. "Denise." He replied

"ok, ok." I got in the car and closed the door. The inside of his car had a comfortable vibe to it. It was black interior with chrome finishing touches. Nice, classy. Nathan pulled off from the store toward the highway.

The ride started off in silence for a moment. A couple of songs played on the radio, Rene & Angela's "Your Smile" now Stephanie Mills. I thought I'd break the silence. I hated awkward silences. It was just as bad as nails on a chalkboard.

"Thanks for the ride Nathan. I really do appreciate it."

"My pleasure, like I said just let me know." He replied. "So is the music ok, you can change it if you want?"

"Oh no, I'm okay, thanks." I declined feeling a little but more comfortable. Nathan nodded.

"Denise."

"Yes, Nathan."

"I'm not sure what's going on in your life now or what you intend to do but I wanted to let you know that I'm here. I care." We stopped at a stop light.

"Thank you for that. I appreciate that you care." I replied not knowing what to make of him and the feelings that I'm having are unexplainable to me right now.

"We can take it slow." He said with a smile.

I gave with a big sigh. "Nathan, it's not you really. It's just that I've been thru a lot and after all that I'm finally at a place where I can give myself the opportunity to trust and be a friend. It's probably gonna be like pulling teeth to be honest. But I'm working on it each day."

"I understand." The light turned green to turn into my neighborhood. "Look, I'll never let you or try to lead you on a path that is not right, ya know. That's not me, I'm not one of those guys. I'm not into all this foolishness that's out here in these streets so don't get the wrong idea." Nathan said this with so much conviction I was a little taken back. But I understood him as well. The worse thing can happen to you is someone judging your character from a shallow lens.

"I do trust you actually. Its me." I replied softly.

"Well…. we'll see. Like I said we can take it slow. I just wanted you to know." Nathan pulled into my driveway and parked. "So, what are you doing tomorrow besides church?"

"Ha, ha!" Nathan often teased me for being such a "church girl." It was my refuge. Without it I'm not sure where I would be so if I believe in the Lord, then "church girl" it is. "I'll probably see what Leah is doing or maybe something else. I really don't have anything planned."

"How about I go with you.?" Nathan asked.

"Where?"

"Church!"

"Umm…"

"Just give me the address and I'll meet you there. Maybe something to eat afterwards if your mom says yes." Nathan added before I could answer. "Yes, I'm persistent, I just like you a lot."

"Let me ask my mom, then I'll let you know alright?"

"Alright." Nathen replied. I stepped out of the car and closed the door. Nathan yelled out the window. "How would you let me know, don't you need my number or something?"

Yes, he is persistent. "Oh, yeah that's right." I said as I turned back to walk toward his car. He had already written it down and had it ready to hand to me thru the window. I took the piece of paper.

"That would have been heartbreaking to not be able to see you tomorrow." He said with a big smile. "See ya later Denise."

"Bye." I went into the house and I heard his SS drive off. Lord what have I gotten myself into.

Chapter 14 [NATHAN]

The very first time I saw Denise I didn't know what to say. She started working at the grocery store about a couple of miles from her neighborhood and about another half mile from my neighborhood. She would walk past me every day without uttering a word. At first, I thought maybe she just was distracted by her own thoughts but then the more I saw her pieces of her started to reveal themselves and I was intrigued. So, I was determined to get to know the lovely Denise Michaels. Every day I would try to speak to her. A whole week and a half passed by before I really got to say more than 3 words to her.

It was a Sunday mid-afternoon. I just came back from helping my dad open for inventory at the shop. I was rushing for my shift at the store as well. I had about 5 minutes left to clock-in before grace time hits. I'm usually on time but for some reason Dad had a lot to talk about. Maybe Mom's giving him the silent treatment. It happens from time to time. It's hilarious to watch them. I arrived just in time with a fast pace when Denise came out of the door where the clock is, and I almost ran into it.

"Oh, I'm so sorry. Did I hit you?" She asked. She had her hands by my face as to embrace the possibility that she did hit me. She did hit me but not in my face. She had the cutest expression of concern. I was in a trace.

"No, no I'm alright." I laughed a little nervously. My eyes felt like they were glossed over with a ray of sunshine when she began to smile out of relief. She began to walk by. "It's just nice to see you again."

She turned around slightly. "I'm sorry, what did you say?" she asked. She made the most adorable face. She made a slight smirk of a smile that revealed her dimples in the corners of her mouth. She was fine. Today was not the day to be off my game.

"It's nice to see you…. again." I replied

"Oh! Yeah…. same to you." She said with a confused look now.

"It's just that I see and speak to you…you know what, it doesn't matter. I gotta go clock in but I'll check you later." I turned to go inside the little area where we clock in. I can see in the reflection of the door mirror she stood there a little longer than needed. That made me nervous that I had messed up my chance trying to make an unnecessary point. *"Good job Nate"* I said to myself as I punched in my code. 15:01 flashed as I pressed the IN button. *"I wonder if she was clocking in or out? She's usually not here on Sundays."* As I walked out the door to head toward the back of the store I glanced to my left and Denise was there at the customer service desk receiving her till. *"Maybe I can talk to her later."* I walked swiftly back to the storage area. I can hear Mr. Wilson loud as ever.

"Has anyone seen Nate?" he yelled from the back.

"I'm right here Mr. Wilson." I said shaking my head.

"Oh, that's a first. Why you late?" he asked more of a pry rather than really concerned about me being "late". I was one of his best workers, so he knew it had to be a good reason. Right?

"Technically I'm within the grace period, I'm good Mr. Wilson." I said lifting a few boxes on the cart to go stock.

"Arrgh! Damn grace period." He mumbled as he walked off. "You know its Sunday; Dairy is coming in."

"No problem Mr. Wilson."

It took me about an hour or sort to sort out the products and head over to the dairy area. I started to stock the butter then the yogurts. Mr. Wilson came back where I was for a price check.

"Here Nate, take this back to register 3 and tell her it's buy one get one free."

"Alright." I walked to the front of the store to register 3. There she was and I immediately melted. I just wanted to touch her. *"What the fuck? How am I gonna get this girl to choose me?"*

I approached the register after taking a deep breath. I handed Denise the butter. She grabbed them both and looked up.

"So, how much are they?" she asked.

"Buy one get one free." I replied.

"Ok, thanks." She rung up the items and told the customer they're total. I lingered around pretending to straighten up the items on the racks by the register. It wasn't that busy today, so I took advantage of the opportunity. After she was done with the customer, I presume she came and stood by me while I was straightening the racks. I must have been really into the role I was playing because it took me a minute to notice she was standing there. It took me by surprise.

"Where is Mr. Wilson?" she asked.

"In the back. He told me to come give you the price." I stood up from "rearranging the racks" and faced her. "I hope that was ok?"

"Oh yeah, I was just expecting him that's all."

"You're usually not here on Sundays." I subliminally asked

"Oh yeah, someone called off, so I just picked up the extra shift. Why not, ya know?!" she provided.

I was in awe of her. I couldn't believe I was standing here, holding a decent conversation I might add. Most of the girls I've been running into so to speak are quite shallow and don't take the time to get to know me. Denise was a breath of fresh air.

"Well, I'll let you get back, I didn't mean to ramble. I got a customer coming." She said backing back to her register.

"No problem, I didn't mind at all." I was on cloud nine. I must have had the biggest grin on my face.

She giggled softly, "Ok, you have a good one." She went about her business with her customer. I walked back to my area thinking about my encounter. I must admit I felt a little better at my chances of going out with Denise. Time will tell and time is what I have for this flower.

Chapter 15 [DENISE]

Nathan and I had a great time at his junior prom. I know I'll be going off to Howard to study Mechanical Engineering and he'll still be here, but we'll see. I haven't talked to Nathan about it yet. Every time I try to bring it up, he "changes the subject" to avoid it. He's sensitive like that. I feel an argument coming on and I'm not really in the mood.

"Really Denise?" he asked

"What?!" I knew it probably WAS the wrong time to say something, but it was subtle not that big of a push for information on some type of assurance or agreement on what we're going to do. "all I asked was are you still going to try to get into Howard or some type of business program near D.C. if I would get in. Is it so bad that I may have a question or two?"

He took a big sigh as we turned on my street. Nate parked on the street instead of my driveway as an indication he had more to say. "No, my love it's not." I loved when he would look upon my adornment and then respected me. It made it harder for him to not be so desirable. "I…I…" he paused a moment and adjusted himself in his seat to face me. "If I talk about it, it becomes a reality and I can't bear it."

"I understand how you're feeling; I'm scared too. I've never done this before or know what this feeling really is. I don't want to hold you from living the beginning of your life, but I don't want to be apart from you either." I expressed with confusion.

"When do you find out if you got in or not or where you going to decide to go?" Nathan asked and I can see the wheels in his head-turning. I must admit I have disobeyed the rules a couple of times to see Nathan. Nothing too bad just sitting in my driveway. I would sneak out my window and go behind the bushes to the side of the house to meet Nate a couple houses down parked. He would flash his lights from high to dim then off in 2-second increments so that I'll know it's him when he saw me. Mom was sleeping so hard because she was pregnant. She decided to be a surrogate for my Dad and his partner. Nate was a friend indeed and I didn't mind taking the risk to see him. "I think we should wait to see where you actually get accepted and then we go from there. Don't take this the wrong way, De-De, I just want to be in the moment now and not think of the possibility of me and you being…." He just paused and shook his head and faced forward with his hand on his head and elbow on the window seal.

"I'm sorry." I moved closer to him and leaned my head on his shoulder. I wrapped my left and right arm around his. He scratched the top of my head and leaned his head on mine.

"Can I kiss you?

"Nathan I'm already 18."

"what do you mean, I can kiss you?"

"Well in my counseling we went over age differences so I can understand more of what happened to me when I was younger. Remember I told you about that." I explained

"Yeah, I remember." He responded

"so, I was just making sure."

"You worry too much, yes there are laws here but we're ok and under God's law I don't believe a kiss will damn your soul to hell."

We both laughed.

For the past year, Nate and I spent a lot of time together. I knew my relationship with Leah would suffer. I cared but I knew I could make it work and lately Leah has been on another vibe. She tends to do that sometimes. It's a side of her that it seems no one could reach. I just let her be.

"I know that silly but you're right, I can overthink things a lot and…."

"A-Lot!" Nate stressed in agreement.

"Alright, leave me alone." I nudged Nathan's shoulder with mine.

We sat there for a moment listening to the radio trying not to look at each other. The connection was overwhelming. I wanted to use my head instead of my heart. I had doubts as well, Nate described exactly how I was feeling. I was just too scared to say, under the assumption that he may not feel the same way. I'm still working on trusting people and not trying to find the hurt before it finds me.

Nathan leaned in closer to my face. He took his hand and lifted my chin so that our lips were aligned. He placed his lips so softly on mine and my heart felt like it exploded. He kissed me again, this time he began to slip his tongue in my mouth. I would stay clear of boys until the day I met Nate, so I've never kissed a boy before. It felt funny at first but the fact that it was him I began to get the feel of it. Nathan leaned in closer and our kisses began to become deeper until a natural sensation to touch him, to let him touch me overcame the moment. We began to lean back, and Nathan's hand began to go up my thigh.

"mm Nate, lets…" I said breathing hard. "let's slow down a little bit." I sat up a little to get my balance.

"yeah…. yeah, yeah my bad." He apologized.

"no, not like that. I need more time."

"Sure. I understand. Got kind of heated." Nathan put his hand around his mouth and revealed a smile.

"Yeah, it did." I lowered my face not in shame but just in thought of what just almost happened. Nathan lifted my chin.

"You alright?" he asked looking into my eyes.

"Yeah"

"don't worry about anything. We'll just pray about it and go from there, ok?"

"Alright!"

I hope I wasn't chasing fool's gold with Nathan. I haven't given my heart totally to Nathan. He always tells me he loves me, but I wouldn't respond with the same gesture.

We were out running the track together for practice outside of school. Nathan was on the track team and I went to try-outs and didn't make the team barely. I wasn't too bummed about it, I just wanted to see how good I was. But I would practice with Nathan some days when I didn't have work or band practice.

"Ok, Cool downtime." Breathing heavily Nathan began to walk with his hands-on-hips then his head but still at a good pace. When running for endurance I'm usually a little behind Nathan so I set the pace to practice his endurance.

"Slow down Geesh." We walked around the track once already. Nathan talking about everything he could think of. I think he missed me. I hadn't seen him for about a week. I went on a band trip and took off from work too. Nathan started to bring up me being gone and the conversation went a different way.

"Oh, my bad, c'mon." he stopped and turned around and waited for me to catch up. He placed his hand on my back to help me along. "So how was your trip?"

"Oh, it was good. We saw some sites and set in on a few sets of different "ghost bands" that were playing. But I'm glad we made it back, that bus ride was intolerable, to say the least." I exclaimed while taking sips of water from Nathan's water bottle while we take our last lap before heading out.

"What happened?" Nathan asked with a little smirk with anticipation that what I was about to say will be a comical moment.

"Well for one, this guy, I think his name is Brody...Brian...I'm not sure. Anyway, he had to sit next to me on the way back and I woke up and he had his hand under my thigh. I grabbed his hand so hard..." I made a twisting motion with my hands.

"Wait...What...he touched you?" Nathan asked

"I took care of it Nathan, please don't. I promise he won't put his hand on anyone else because I almost broke every finger on his hand." I firmly assured Nathan.

"I'm just saying De-De, if anything would happen to you...." Nathan took a pause. "I'm still gonna find out who that dude is."

"Nate, I told you..."

"I don't care, I love you." Nate blurted out.

I stopped in mid-stride of walking. "What did you say?"

"Uh, nothing. Just keep walking." He avoided

"No, let's not keep walking." I tugged on Nate's shoulder as he began to walk off to stop him. "Did you just say what I think you said?"

Annoyed Nathan answered. "Yeah, Denise. I didn't mean to say it...well, I do or did but...I've been meaning to tell you.... I just didn't want to tell you this way." Nate rubbed his head in frustration.

"Why are you acting like it's a bad thing to say?"

"It's not De-De, I just didn't want to tell you LIKE this. That's all. I just had this picture in mind of how it would be when I tell you."

"Wow, Nate I don't know what to say." Still surprised. Then he told me something I would never forget about love.

"You don't have to say anything. I love you and that's it. If you don't or do feel the same way, it doesn't matter to me. I love you because of who you are not based on how you feel about me."

Maybe everything will work out just fine. Lord knows this past year has been the happiest I have been in a while. If he so grants Nathan and I to continue or if there are obstacles for that to happen then so be it. Who is to say what the future holds? The unexplainable events in my life that have already taken place, from when I was younger to now, has taught me I am not in control of my life. I have free will but not the master plan of it all.

Chapter 16 [LEAH]

"Get yo hands off me. Don't touch me." I said with my fist clinched back ready to clock Lewis in his mouth.

"Stop trippin' Leah! What am I supposed to say?" he said in frustration, fear, and confusion.

Here we are arguing again and today I must tell him that I know the reason why. You see I continued to get rides from Lewis from work and school from time to time. This turned into a regular thing. Lewis and I are just friends, but things have turned sour in our friendship when we decided to sleep together about 2 months before prom. I decided not to go to my prom because I found out I was pregnant. I've been hiding it from Lewis for some time. I finally told my mother about a week after I found out. She didn't seem to be surprised.

"I knew somebody was pregnant. I dreamed of fish last night." Mama said.

"oh, mama I've messed up. I had the mindset; I really did but…What am I gonna do?" I cried. "Lord forgive me."

"Leah, the Lord is merciful and forgiving. We just gotta sit down here and see what's the next step. Who's the father?" she asked.

"Who's the father?!!" I said feeling insulted. "How many boys you think I have been with, mom?"

"One, lower your voice. You go in and out of here Leah like it's no tomorrow. Even though you're always here at a

decent hour and I try to believe that you are telling the truth about where you say you really are…wait…two there's the incident where you said you were at work but come to find out you really left early and went to a coworkers house."

"Mom! I wasn't feeling too good and I didn't want to stand in the heat. She was getting off already, so I got a ride." I explained again

"What, you didn't realize you were not in your own home chile?" she asked sarcastically. "and why should I believe you, Leah. Chile, I don't know what I'm gonna do with you. You wait right at the end of your senior year. Lord!" She got up from the couch toward the kitchen. I sat there a moment blowing my nose continuously which was a result of my minor breakdown. Mom came back with a glass of milk. It was a little warm to calm my nerves. This always helped when I was sad, I'm not sure why. Any other time I drink milk I usually would put an ice cube in it so it can be cold. "Here you go."

"Thank you," I said. Mom sighed and sat back on the couch and folded her arms. It looks like the wheels were turning in her head. "Mama, I'm so sorry, I didn't mean for this to happen."

"I know honey, I know"

Well, after talking to mama some more. We felt it was best to involve Lewis as well. I told mama I would talk to him alone first, but I've been dodging any contact with him for weeks. I finally got the nerve to call him back. Of course, this was the hardest thing I've had to do thus far. I mean I just graduated high school. I have my job at the record store but I'm not sure what type of father Lewis will be. I asked Lewis to meet me by the bus stop one street over from my house. I waited a while before I headed out. Mama was at work and I know this was a good time to meet up with him without hearing her mouth about my every move. Lewis had just pulled up to the side by the bus stop to park when he looked up and saw me walking toward him. He got out the car, but I didn't look up at him. I kept going to the passenger side of his car, opened the door and got in. Lewis got in after I did. He closed the door slowly as if he was not in a rush to hear what had to be said. I got straight to the point. I told Lewis about my pregnancy and showed him my stomach where I was starting to show a little. I was a little over 12 weeks now.

"NOT 'ARE YOU GONNA KEEP IT'!" I yelled. I was so angry not at Lewis but myself. I should have known better. Why didn't I think? I let one kiss throw me completely out of my box with this guy. I felt weak, stupid and hopeless all at once. How can something that seems to happen so naturally can be the very thing that can break up a completely good friendship?

We both sat there in silence for a few minutes. The thoughts of the afternoon in question going over and over in my head was like the torture of my transgression:

"Nice room Lewis but yeah…I expected it to be like this." I teased

"And what does that supposed to mean?" Lewis looked up from tying his shoes. We were coming back from one of Lewis's basketball games. He wanted to take a shower before we head back out to get something to eat. It was Saturday afternoon. I asked Lewis where his parents were. He said his mom and dad went to run errands before coming back home. They were at the game cheering, loudly. It was nice to see Lewis have supportive parents.

"I mean you've always been neat. Geesh! You're sure are sensitive today."

"mm-hmm"

I'm not sure what the animosity was about but I wasn't for it today. Lewis had been acting weird for the past couple of months now.

"What's going on with you, Lewis?" I asked as he walked over to his closet for a belt. He had just taken a shower and came back to put on the last touches of his "gear." "...because you've been acting weird for a couple of months now."

"Have you been talking to James?" he blurted out as he turned away from the closet.

"Yes. We spoke once or twice in the hall. I mean, I do know him, Lewis. Why?" I was confused but then again, to be honest, I wasn't.

I knew Lewis wanted more. As I sit here in his room gazing at his every move, I really noticed "him" I can't explain it, but I got a better understanding of his personality in the way he walked back and forth and now how adorable he is to me as his jealousy decides to take center stage. From my experience with jealous guys, I'm not sure if that's a good sign. I didn't trust Lewis enough to be more than just friends. But, after today at this very moment, I was flattered. He's an attractive guy. Lewis was tall, well taller than me. He stood a little over 6ft to my 5"5' stature. Being with him platonically did feel safe. The days where we are just hanging out at the record store listening to music have been some of my better days. He would "accidentally" grab the top of my hand when reaching for a record. Or his hugs of hello and goodbye are just a little bit too long. Sometimes it's hilarious and annoying on how he just won't give up. The more time I spend with him though, I do find myself thinking about him in a more romantic way.

"Nothing, Leah." He said agitatedly. "Let's go."

"Ok, let's go. You don't have to talk about it." I got up from the chair I was sitting in to head toward the door. Lewis turned toward me so fast it made me jump. "what's wrong with you?" startled, to say the least.

"That's what I'm talking about Leah. This nonchalant, I don't care attitude of yours is getting old. You know damn well why I'm asking." He was in my face at this point. I can feel the breath from his nostrils. "Stop playing with me."

"Ok, first of all...back...up." I almost had a flashback of the beatings I used to see my mom get from her boyfriends or whomever, so I was a little nervous. "Secondly, why should it bother you Lewis when we are not together, he's

not my boyfriend and for God's sake don't act like you haven't been with God knows who."

"Oh, c'mon really, are we going back to this now. You're still judging me. I haven't shown you anything like that." He proclaimed.

"And I suppose to just believe it DOESN'T happen." I snapped back. I tried every sarcastic thing to get Lewis to back off the subject, but I knew he was too determined.

"You know what I believe?"

"What's that Lewis?" I said sarcastically.

"You want me with someone else, that way you don't have to admit it to yourself."

"Admit what?"

"You're afraid, Leah. You're a coward." He threw his keys on his desk. He walked over to the bed and sat down and began taking off his shoes.

"What are you doing, we have to go to remember?" I reminded him but was upset that I knew he was bummed out about me talking to James.

"Leah, I'm really not in the mood."

"What for food?" there was no answer. He sat there looking straight ahead with the most blank look on his face. "Oh! Not in the mood for me, that's what you're trying to say?" He turned and looked at me. "I get the hint." I grabbed my jacket and headed toward the door again.

"Leah!" Lewis got up and grabbed my arm and pulled me back.

"No, let me go Lewis," I said tussling from his minor grip.

"C'mon just stop." Lewis was blocking the door. He still had me and pulled me closer. He grabbed my face with both his hands. "Come here." He said softly as he kissed me slowly. He brought me closer as the intensity of our kisses overlapped. Lewis was a year older than me and a little more experienced. I was so nervous. Before I knew it, we were on the bed and Lewis kissing me all over. I mean he even kissed and licked my kneecaps. "I want you." He said as he started to unbutton my blouse.

He had this alluring look in his eyes that caught me off guard and there was no turning back now. I filled with his energy; I began to kiss Lewis. He ripped my skirt and blouse off. He climbed on top of me after gazing on my body. I didn't feel ashamed. He began to caress my clitoris while sucking on my breast. And I let him. I desired Lewis just as much as he wanted me. Lewis leaned over to his side drawer. He pulled out a condom. He got up from the bed, unbuttoned and took off his pants and shirt. I turned to look at his "love" and I'm not sure what is a good size or not but from the looks of it, this is not going to be easy. He slid his condom on and climbed back into bed with me.

"I know it's your first time, so just let me know…" he said rubbing the top of my forehead as if he was moving hair out the way.

"Yeah, ok."

We began to kiss and caress each other's bodies. I was so hot and ready to receive him. He began to penetrate inside me, and it hurt like no other.

"Ouch! Yeah, yeah that hurts."

"Ok, Ok," Lewis reassured me. He kissed me on the cheek and pulled out a little. He continued to go back and forth, and I can feel his breath on my neck and face. "I'll take it slow." I can feel Lewis tongue in my ear. The more he went back and forth the deeper inside me he went until he was fully in me. This is where he took one last thrust. "SHIT!"

I stop breathing for a quick second. "Ahh."

"You ok?"

"Yes. Yes."

I couldn't believe I had lost my virginity to Lewis. Of all people, I would have thought James. It's funny who you "fall in love" with. Even though we were young I do believe what I feel for Lewis is real, even if I don't want to admit it. Maybe he was right. I am a coward. Running away from love has proved to not work out well. In the end the heart wants what the heart wants and that day I made the decision to surrender to love.

"Leah. Despite what you may be thinking, I do care and I… I do love…you. I love you." Lewis struggled to say. I'm not sure if he was unsure or was just didn't know what to say. I know he cared for me but love me, that's still under review. "We'll figure this out. I have some money saved up and I already work with my dad for now." He grabbed my hand and held it firmly. "It's ok, just trust me."

Chapter 17 [JAMES]

"OMG, did you hear that Leah is pregnant?" Marissa was in my dorm room after we just had another "make-up" session after one of the many arguments we have each week. We ended up at Prairie View together not far from where we grew up in Hempstead. I got a basketball scholarship and was studying psychology and Marissa was in the nursing program. I hadn't heard from Leah in a while. Last I knew about her was that she and Lewis had moved in together. I won't say that I don't hold a candle for Leah still, but I gave up on that dream a long time ago.

Marissa came into the picture on accident, she was just someone that so happen to be there. That day in the record store when Leah saw me and Marissa together, I was not interested in Marissa. She just seemed to have become attached to me somehow. Truly the sex is good, but it just wasn't happening.

"Uh, no. No, I didn't hear that? I replied putting back on my shirt. Hopefully, Marissa will get the hint and get ready to go. Just hearing "Leah is pregnant" knowing I've never experienced the chance to show Leah how much I need and want her almost made me give up the ghost. I began to overheat and breathe a little deeper. Lost love can take your breath away just as quick as love found.

Shaking her head. "A shame. You lie down with dogs; you're bound to come up with flees." As always, she always had a sharp tongue when it came to Leah. Marissa and Leah have been going at it since grade school. I really don't know what the issue is but it's becoming obsessive. "I'm not surprised anyway." She continued.

"Ok, can you just cool it. You don't know the situation." Marissa knew how I felt about Leah. Maybe that's why she seems to create this dark cloud over Leah's head when speaking of her existence every chance she gets.

"What? I'm just saying."

"Yeah, but it's becoming annoying," I added. Marissa looked up from the magazine she was casually flipping through. She placed the magazine on the bed and got up to start putting on her clothes. "What?"

"Nothing."

"Here we go," I said under my breath.

"Ha! You know what James; I'll check you later." She picked up her keys and purse and headed toward the door. She stopped; turned around. "And for your information, the jab was at Lewis, not Leah." She slammed the door.

Always some drama. Since day one, what she wants, she gets and there is no stopping her. Marissa and I grew up next door to each other. She was this innocent preacher's kid with braces and glasses. Every time I would see her, I thought she was quite quirky. She had a shy sense about her. Never had her head held up for people to see her face. I believe the first time I really noticed Marissa was when I was going into the grocery store with my Mom and Dad after church. I believe I was around 12 or 13 years old at the time. We were coming in and she and her Mom and

Dad were coming out with just a bag or two. It looked like they had the same idea we did. On Sundays sometimes we stop and pick up chicken or some other hot dish if Mom didn't feel like cooking.

"Hey, how are you doing?" My Dad waved to the Orville's as we approached.

"Oh, Afternoon" "Hello" "Good, Good." Everyone exchanged greetings except for me and Marissa. She was standing there with her hands behind her back and one leg over the other. She had on a white ivory dress with a white flower on the side of her textured afro. Her eyebrows were of a deep brown that brought out the essence in light brown eyes. Her lips looked like they were stained by the kiss of a rose that brought a flush to her cheeks upon her caramel skin. I licked my lips as if I could taste them.

"JAMES!"

I didn't realize my mom had called my name a few times while I was on the verge of exploding in my pants. "Wha-huh?" I tried to respond.

"Are you gonna say hi son?" my mom laughed out of embarrassment looking at the Orville's as she apologized with her eyes.

"Hello," she said and held out her hand for me to shake. Marissa was no longer that quirky girl with the glasses and braces I used to see with her head held down. She was confident, beautiful and with a bold presence that I haven't experienced. I was intrigued. I reached out to shake her hand. My palms were sweaty and all I could imagine in my

head was her face after encountering the wet nastiness that was coming out of my pores.

"Hi," I said trying not to sound more ridiculous than I had looked just a few minutes ago.

My Dad laughed. "Teenage boys." They all laughed a little as if they were the only ones with the secret and no one else knew.

I lusted for Marissa then and I lust for her now. The reason I say lust is that I still have feelings for Leah and Marissa knows that. Leah was that girl that just does it for me. I'm in a place of calm that I have never been before. We were both unable to get to a place where we could just ask each other what we wanted from each other. Before I knew it, Marissa was in my face and I fell for the easy way out instead of falling for love. You see, I knew Lewis was pursuing Leah when I saw them walk into school that morning. I couldn't believe it. It broke my heart. I mean Lewis has always said he was interested in Leah in passing but I never told him of my feelings. Who am I to step in a brotha's way, that's the game? It's up to her to choose at the end of the day and that day it looks like she made her choice. She barely looked at me:

"Hey, Leah!?" I said her name so loud it caught me off guard.

"Oh, Hey James." she did a short wave and kept walking with Lewis. Lewis gave me a quick nod as if he was claiming her.

I wanted to talk to Leah about what happened, so I prepared to face the music. I said a quick bye to my homies and walked down the hall toward Leah's' locker. She blew me off. I was so let down that dating anyone was not of importance anymore until Marissa approached me. She was seductive and convincing so why not. It's just sex until someone starts catching feelings. I want to be honest with Marissa and tell her that I just want to be friends and see other people. But I'm afraid that will not go over so well, especially since I'm still in love with Leah and that's where she will take the conversation. I know it.

Hearing that Leah is now pregnant really took me to another dimension. Apart of me wants to call her up and check up on her and then another part of me is still angry at how things were left between us. Knowing Lewis, he will try to claim it's not his.

Lewis and I have been on rocky ground ever since freshman year in high school when he did some gutter shit to me over a girl. It was one of those who really wanted me but went through Lewis. He thought I tried to push up on the duck, but my eyes were set on Leah from the first day I saw her walk in the school. Lewis knowing this left a note in Leah's locker about the girl out of spite. I should of kick his ass, but he wasn't worth it. Lewis always wants what he can't have and now him being the father of Leah's baby just makes me angrier than I've been in a while.

"I can't believe this," I said to myself after Marissa left. I sat on the edge of my bed with my face in my hands as I rubbed back and forth trying the process the news I just got. I almost wanted to cry but I didn't. I leaned back on my bed and thought about the make-up sex I was going to have with Marissa later when she comes begging. That'll help shake it off, hopefully.

She always comes back ever since the summer going into our 11th-grade year. After Leah in my eyes "dumped me" I was crushed. I tried talking to her a couple of times but no success. Feeling hopeless I fled to my next option. It was not the prototype just a replacement of what Leah carved out of my heart without letting me explain.

Marissa started lingering around more outside of her house with her friends. She had really "filled out" if you know what I mean; I was aroused. On this day, Dad was inside going back and forth with Mom about where I'll be going to school. Those two never quit. I went outside to catch a breeze and there she was sitting on the back on her Dad's pick-up truck. I watched as she jumped off the back to the ground hoping her sundress will fly up just enough to see how much ass is back there. Now I've scoped out older girls and even grown women with the homies while out and about but for a mere 17 Marissa had an onion. An ass that'll make a brotha damn near cry. I didn't know that much about her like interest, hobbies; just that she went to church a lot and her Mom and Dad were very strict.

She turned around and looked my way. She put her hand on her hips and the sexiness that she possessed was alluring and easy to give in to. I knew I should have just walked away that day, but I thought, *"what the hell?!"* With her girlfriends in the background she sashayed a few more steps down the sidewalk:

"Is it something you need to say?" Marissa asked.

"About?"

"I don't know but by the way you are staring, something must be on your mind." She had a sassiness about her that was a turn on. She turned to look at her girlfriends and giggled a little. "every day I see you spying on me James but I'm sure Leah wouldn't appreciate that now would she?"

"And why would you care what Leah would appreciate or not?" I asked knowing that would sting a little. The rivalry between the two of them has been going on forever.

"I DON'T."

"Well ok, wus up then?" I stepped closer to her. Just enough to get a hint of her scent. The wind blew at the perfect time refreshing me with her scent as she struggled with her dress so it wouldn't fly away from her body.

"With what?" she paused for a minute and her whole expression changed. "Oh, I see, you want some ass, don't you?"

"I didn't say that."

"Yeah, but you were thinking it. You don't have the foggiest idea about me, yet you judge me off rumors."

She was getting intense and the look on her face had told me I better tread softly. "I never said any of that, Marissa. Why are you getting upset at a simple hello?" I asked.

Marissa looked like she came back down to earth for a minute. Where she went, I'm not sure but, I still found her very attractive. "Well, I'm just used to guys...never mind." She looked at her girlfriends and back at me. "I have to go, bye."

She turned and walked back toward her house. I watched as her hips and ass move like African drums under that sundress that was fitting her ever so nicely. Marissa looked exotic. Her dark bronze skin just glistened as the sun brought about a kiss of gold to highlight the defining lines of her legs, arms, and cheeks. She was fair to look upon as well. The curls of her hair blew in the wind so naturally and flawlessly as she got back on her Dad's pickup truck. She WAS beautiful.

Later, that night while lying in bed, I couldn't get Marissa off my mind. The way she looked earlier that just kept reoccurring in my mind. I got up out of the bed and went to wash my face and teeth again. I drunk some sips from the faucet thinking this would help but it didn't. I got in the shower and rinsed off for about 15 minutes hoping this would cool down the explosion of hormones raging inside of me for Marissa. I got out the shower and dried off. I lotioned my body, put on a t-shirt and basketball pants and slipped on my slippers. I went downstairs to get something to eat but for some reason, I grabbed my jacket and headed out the door. I stood outside for a moment contemplating if I should see if Marissa is up or not. Her mom usually works a double on Saturdays at the hospital since her parents split. I hesitated, then I thought to myself: *"Fuck it!"* I ducked low and ran over to the side of the house where Marissa's room is. I found this out when we were younger when my mom and her mom used to hang out at each other's houses. They don't hang out so much now, as a matter of fact.

I found my way to Marissa's window and checked to see if it was unlocked. "Dammit." It wasn't. I covered the top of my forehead to block the glare from the security lights Marissa's Dad put up a while back, to see if she was up. I saw her move a little in her bed. I began to tap on her window loud enough for her to hear but not loud enough to cause a commotion. The neighbors in our hood are nosey. That's all I need is for someone to catch me out here in the middle of the night. I tapped some more until I finally saw her stirring around. TAP! -TAP! She sat up and looked around for a bit until her big dark black eyes were set in my direction piercing me in my chest. Her hair was all over the place, but she was still beautiful. I thought "damn!" I signaled for her to open the window. She looked hesitant for a minute by her gestures of confusion of why I was there in the first place. She got up and walked to the other side of the room. She had on a white nightgown, but the light hit her breast so right I could see her dark brown nipples speaking out at me to caress them. She put on her robe and finally gave in and came to the window. She unlatched it and I helped her push it up. She stuck her head out and tightened her rose-colored provocative lips in skepticism.

"What are you doing, it's the middle of the night?" she whispered.

"I know, I just wanted to talk to…" we both heard a noise coming from down the side of the house where her neighbor's side door is.

"Is somebody out there?" a lady called out. That was Ms. James the neighborhood gossip.

"Shit, shit help me up!" I reached for Marissa to grab my arms while I hopped through the window.

"Oh, Jes-! Hold on a minute. Ugghh!" Marissa got me in just in time. "Okay, get down." I sat on the floor under the window while she closed it slowly and quietly. She closed the window curtains so she could look without being noticed. I stayed as still as possible. "She's gone. Nosey bat always lurking. Now, what do you want?"

"I'm sorry Marissa about earlier," I got up from the floor to say what I had to say better. "I didn't mean to insinuate that...well...I didn't mean to come off disrespectful."

"So, you come and wake me up in the middle of the night to say that?" she asked skeptically

"Yes, you seemed upset and that's the last thing I want to do. C'mon Marissa we've known each other for a long time, I can't be as bad as I seem to be. I do care." I said trying to make her understand.

"Well, I guess. Thanks, James" she readjusted her robe and folded her arms. I stood there just gazing at her not knowing what to say next. "What?" she asked with a smirk.

"Nothing...I just noticed you have a dimple on your right cheek." The light from outside was lit across her face. "You're beautiful."

"Oh, stop it James." she walked over to the edge of her bed and sat down. "You really think so?"

"Yeah! You don't?" I asked in confusion. Has she even looked in a mirror? I sat next to her thinking maybe I don't know anything about her. Here I am thinking Marissa was this stuck up, "my shit doesn't stink," mean girl when really, she was just a lonely girl who felt trapped in her own skin because society views you by your appearance than who you truly are. She was very insecure.

"Boys only want one thing from me. They take one look at me and forget I have a brain and feelings."

I began to feel a little guilty of all the sexual thoughts I did have of Marissa. I mean it's not like I knew this was going on with her. Yet and still I felt sympathy for her. "I'm not going to lie to you Marissa, I'm attracted to you, but it doesn't mean I don't realize there is more to you than just that." I got up from the bed to walk toward the window. "And you need to realize that too, people only treat you the way you allow them to." I moved the curtains to see if Ms. James had gone back in and if was alright to go out the window. As I was peeking out the window the curtains suddenly closed. I moved my head back to see Marissa standing on the side of me with just her gown on. She began to take my jacket off until it fell on the floor effortlessly. She came closer and placed her hands on my face. At this moment her touch sent shocks straight thru me. I was quickly aroused. She pulled me closer and placed her lips on mine. The same rose-colored lips that were full of intensity when I first arrived were now relaxed and supple to the touch. I gave in. I grabbed her and held her tightly as

I began to deepen the kiss between us. Those kisses went deeper and deeper until I adventured to other places I could explore on her body. We navigated toward her bed. As I lay on top of her making sure I touch every part of her, I couldn't help but notice the intense passion of us being together. I lifted her and helped her out of her gown, and she laid back on the bed exposing those breasts I saw in the light by the window. Believe me the light didn't give their beauty justice. I started to caress and suck with great intensity. Before I knew it, I was inside of Marissa and she received me with ease. She felt so good as I built up the intensity of each thrust and she moaned in satisfaction.

Chapter 18 [DENISE]

Arriving at Howard University was exciting and nerve-wrecking at the same time. First, they didn't have my resident hall assignment, when I sent in the fee to hold my spot months ago, so my mom handled that with a swiftness. Mom and Dad helped me get settled in my room along with Nate. Nate ended up getting into Georgetown on a track scholarship. I was so happy when he told me the news, I didn't know what to do with myself.

"What? You're joking, right? aaahhhhhhhh!" I jumped on Nate and hugged him so tight I think I may have cut off his air supply.

"Babe, babe I…can't breathe!" he said laughing as I let go.

"Oh, I'm sorry!" I grabbed his face and placed my forehead on his. We kissed. "You okay?"

"Yeah, I'm okay." He looked so happy while rubbing the side of his neck.

I knew this was going to be a hard transition for Nate and me with me being here for a year before he starts attending Georgetown. But I didn't care I was on cloud nine and nothing could dampen my mood.

"Ok, honey is that all your stuff?" Mom asked

"Yeah, I think so. Oh, Nate is bringing in one more thing." I remembered.

"Alright, that should hold," Dad said as he finished hanging the last of my posters and pictures I brought. "Ok, baby girl. You're all set."

"Thanks, Daddy."

"Your welcome. I'm so proud of you. You call if you need anything De-De, I mean it." He was hugging me so tight like it was going to be the last time he will ever see me.

"I will dad, don't worry." Nate walked in with the last of my things. "Oh, I was wondering if you would find your way."

"oh yeah, no problem. This is everything so…." Nate looked around at everyone. I could feel the bright spirit he had earlier just dim in his realization of reality. "can Leah and I have a few minutes please?"

"Oh sure, sure." Dad gave me a kiss on the forehead. "C'mon Mi-Mi, let them have their moment."

"Alright. Oh, Come here my love. I'm gonna miss you so much." Mom said as she hugged me tightly.

"I'll miss you to mom," I replied

"Nate we'll be waiting down by the car when you finish, ok?" mom said as she and Dad headed toward the door.

"Ok, Ms. Michaels thanks. I promise I won't be that long."

"Take your time," Dad reassured him.

"Bye, baby." Mom said waving as the door closed.

I already knew Nathan wanted reassurance that everything was going to be alright with us. I can understand it. I had my doubts and anxieties as well. We were young and just starting out with our adult lives and nothing feels better than to have someone to go on this type of journey with.

"Hey," Nathan said. The look on his face showed the words he wanted to say but he couldn't express them.

"Hey," I responded.

He took a deep breath and walked toward me. He pulled my hair back from my face and looked upon my face for which seemed forever. I broke the silence by letting a stream of tears fall from my eyes.

"Stop crying De-De, please don't make it any harder. I'm just a call away and we have the holidays and spring break. We'll see each other before you know it."

"I know. It still hurts Nate. I'm going to miss you so much." I said with my tears blurring my vision as they continued to fall down my cheeks and beyond.

Nate and I must have stood in the middle of my dorm room and hugged each other for an eternity. How can this be the happiest and saddest day of my life? I didn't want to let him go but I knew I had to sooner or later. Nate took his arms from around me and held my hands.

"I love you, Denise."

"Love you too."

"I'll call you when I make it back home, ok. No worries."

I shook my head in agreement as we walked toward the door to meet my parents. We all walked outside and said I final goodbyes. I stood on the steps of the dorm and watched as they walked toward the parking lot until they were out of sight. They were gone. I felt alone but not lonely. I went back inside and walked around a little to check out the dorm. I saw a group of students in the lounge area and wanted to go mingle to get my mind off today and the hours that will have to pass before I hear from Nate again. I changed my mind and went back to my room instead. I sat on the edge of my bed staring out the window. My roommate wasn't here yet, so I had the room to myself for now. I started to put away the things that Nate brought in the box but couldn't get through it before I completely lost it and started to cry uncontrollably. This was going to be harder than I thought. I've never been this far away from home before. Away from the familiar and comfortable. I sobbed until I fell asleep.

Chapter 19 [JAMES]

I had to pay my dues to Ms. Moses to get Leah's number to call her. Marissa said she went to go see Leah in the hospital after she had the baby. I believe it was a boy. As I sat on the edge of my bed rocking back and forth contemplating if I should call Leah or not, I began to recall the last time I talked to Leah. It was the end of our 11th-grade year.

I was at basketball camp most of the summer so, everything was pretty routine for me; Get up, eat, practice, eat, practice, sleep, work and sometimes not in that order; until one day I decided to take a stroll instead of sleeping when I had the day off from work like I usually do. I ended up down the strip mall area where Leah used to work at the record store. As I approached my curiosity started to flow through my veins of wondering if she still worked there or does, she comes in from time to time. As I approached, I couldn't help myself, I peeked through the window of the store to see if I could spot any sign of Leah. There were a few people there, but I couldn't really tell who was working in the store. I felt a tap on my shoulder that startled me so that I thought I swallowed my heart:

"Looking for something?" she said. The beauty that stood in front of me gave me the energy of sophistication as her jeans showed off those voluptuous hips that would put you in a hypnotic state without evening swaying back and forth. All I wanted to do was grab her waist and pull her close to me and transport back to where things were rearranged to place me and her being together in this moment.

"Hey…um…I guess you caught me." I said out of embarrassment of my hidden secret of being an under-cover stalker. Leah's skinned glistened under the sunny day that was upon us. Her dark chocolate skin looked like it was made from silk and God decided to add a glimpse of his light in every kiss of the sun upon her.

She shook her head as she opened the door to the store. "James, I swear." She laughed a little as she entered the store with me trailing right behind her.

"Leah, look I just want to try and explain this time. Every time I try, you…"

"I what?" she interrupted.

"That, Leah. That. Can I at least try to explain then you don't have to ever see me again if you desire?" I begged. I needed to do this. I needed to know how she really felt about me. What she thought mattered.

"Fine James. I have about seven minutes before I start my shift, so make it quick." We started to walk toward the back of the store where all the storage was kept. Leah spoke to a few people and then walked a little further. "C'mon this way." We went outside a side door that led to the side of the strip mall closer to the parking lot. "Ok, go ahead James." Leah rambled through her purse before putting it back over her shoulder and folded her arms to listen. For some reason I just loved the way she looks when she tries to not show she is upset.

"She's not my girlfriend," I exclaimed

"Oh, Please James. But does it matter, we're not together? Why you feel the need to explain?" She snapped a little. I knew that was coming. Leah never had any issue with expressing how she felt regardless of the barrier she tried to put up around her heart.

"Because I care about you and I care about your feelings. You know I've been trying to get closer to you, but it just seems you not with that." I moved closer to Leah. "But I'll never stop trying." I moved Leah's hair away from her forehead.

"Stop James." She slapped my hand away. "I'm seeing Lewis."

"Yeah, don't I know that. Good one by the way." I couldn't stand to hear her say those words. The thought of her and Lewis just made me cringe with bitterness.

"What are you talking about now James?" she asked nonchalantly

"You know how I, and Lewis feel about each other, c'mon. So, what, you decided to start hanging or going out with him to prove what Leah? You never gave me a chance to explain." I stressed this constantly.

"James, you see that's your problem. You think it's all about you."

That hurt me deep in my heart in a way that I have never experienced. I guess it was all part of growing up and Leah didn't mind contributing her aspect with her sound words. I did have to admit I didn't give too much effort on telling

Leah how I really felt about her. I can understand the tentative behavior I was demonstrating did not help me, which is why I'm in this situation as it is. "Look, Leah, I never meant to lead you on or hurt you in any type of way. I should have been more upfront on how I feel about you. I was just afraid of rejection. You're so beautiful and you can have anybody you want. You're my best friend. And now I think I may have messed that up somehow."

"We both did. Let's just let bygones be bygones and move on. You will always be my friend James." She said so sweetly as if she just kissed my ear with her lips that seem to reflect the color of her rose-colored blouse. Her hair blew in the wind as feathers on the wings of a bird and I could smell her perfume as it engulfed me to remind me of how it was to see her beauty for the very first time which seemed so long ago.

Sadly, this is not what I wanted to hear. I know I had to respect her boundaries but as far as I was concerned Leah was mine and mine only and however long it took for us to be together, I was willing to wait. "I love you, Leah, I always will. If you need anything..." I looked at her one last time so that I may remember every curve of her face. The frown marks on her forehead that I touch so slightly so she may relax her precious mind. "If you need anything, I'm always here."

I dialed the number that Ms. Moses gave me. It appears that Leah is with Lewis in their new apartment that his parents are renting for them now. I didn't know what to expect but I wasn't going to let the fact that she is living with Lewis stop me from checking on her. They're not married. The phone was still ringing.

RING! I sighed in relief thinking that maybe no one was home, and I can leave a message. That way I wouldn't have to go through the awkwardness of this call. I was mistaken.

"Hello!" I can hear the coos of a baby in the background. "Hello?" she said again. I knew it was Leah by her voice. She sounded a little tired, but I can still hear the sweetness that I've longed to hear from her lips.

"Uh, yes. Can I speak to Leah Anders please?" I didn't just want to call as if I did all the time and I knew it was her.

"May I ask who's calling?" she asked skeptically.

"Uh yes, this is James Deitrick."

"Oh! Hi James! How are you?" she asked with a little perk in her voice. That was surprising to me. I was sure I was going to get the cold shoulder.

"I'm okay. Just calling to check up on you. I got your number from your mom. I hope you don't mind?" I asked nervously.

"Oh no, not at all. I'm okay just a little occupied over here." She said with a slight laugh.

"Yeah, I can hear, congratulations Leah." It was a bittersweet emotion towards Leah's situation. I couldn't believe that it was a reality that there maybe will not be a chance to win Leah's heart back.

"Thanks, and thank you for calling, I appreciate you thinking about me." She said. I wanted to go into the details of her life. I wanted her to tell me she was in a situation but still thought of me. I wanted to be in her life. I felt she needed me being so young and with this responsibility, I just didn't think ol' boy would be able to do it.

"Always, I'm here." I took a deep sigh. "Well, I'll let you goooo." I said with a slight laugh to lighten the mood. "You take care of that little one, I know you'll be a great mom."

"Okay, thanks, James."

"No problem, bye Leah."

"Bye." I waited until she hung up the phone. So many emotions came over me in that one moment. My chance with Leah was gone. As tears, that seemed to want to push thru regardless of how strong my pride tried to hold them back, began to stream down my face; I hung up the phone and laid back on my dorm room bed and sobbed.

Chapter 20 [DENISE]

It's been almost 3 months since I've been home from school. D.C. in the wintertime is not something I am used to, being from Texas. I adjusted well after my breakdown at the beginning of the semester and was able to function after I got it all out. My roommate finally made it in from Chicago. We get along pretty good. She stays out of my way and me out of hers. Every now and again I would hang out with her. She was really into her boyfriend and the social scene. I am more of a loner now. I just want to focus on my studies and anticipate the day that Nathan moves out this way. My Dad bought a plane ticket for me to fly back home for Thanksgiving break. I couldn't wait to get some real southern food for a change.

My plane landed on time and I was able to retrieve all my belongings from baggage claim. I went out to the passenger pick up area and spotted my Mom and Dad waiting in the line of cars for passengers. I walked up to the side of the car on the passenger side and did a quick tap on the window.

[MUFFLED] "Oh my goodness!" my mom said as she turned to see me outside of the car door. She struggled to open the door at first. I can tell she was overly excited. It was hilarious. My Dad was already out of the car as soon as my Mom was able to open the car door

"Baby girl!" my dad trotted around to the other side of the car and gave me the biggest hug. I could hardly breathe.

"Arrgh, Dad…I. Cant. Breath!" I struggled to say.

"Move, let me hug my baby." My mom playfully shoved my Dad out of the way. I hugged my Mom so tightly. I missed her so much. My Dad put my bags in the trunk as Mom and I continued to greet each other, laughing and checking out each other's outfits. We finally got in the car and was on our way leaving the airport. It felt good to be back home. There was a lot more construction at the airport than before. Bush Intercontinental was the closest airport to fly into from Hempstead. It'll be an hour before we made it home and an hour of listening to my Mom and Dad go back and forth like rivaling siblings. "Paul, that's the wrong way!" mom said pointing toward the opposite direction that my dad went, "It's that way."

"Minnie, I got this," Dad replied.

I can't wait to see Nathan and tell him all about the last few months. We've been playing phone tag for a couple of weeks now, but I won't make a fuss about it. Everything takes time. We finally got to the house and I unpacked my luggage. I could smell the scent of pumpkin spice scented candles mixed with home cooking. My mom always started cooking the day before Thanksgiving. It made it easier the day of when the family comes by. I helped Mom in the kitchen with dinner with a little girl chit chat to go with it. I didn't know how attached I was to my mother until I had to leave for the past few months. You really don't know what you have until it's not readily available or worse, gone.

"so how are you adjusting, De-De?" mom asked as she put the final dishes in the cabinets.

"You know, it's been going a lot smoother than I thought. My roommate is nice. Everything is ok mom." I placed my head on her shoulder and gave her a slight arm hug.

"Oh, I know honey. That's one thing I know I can do is trust you. So, let's keep that going." She chuckled.

"Yes Ma'am," I said jokingly as if I was a soldier. I even gave her a little salute. We joked around like that a lot. Laughter was always the medicine we could afford.

After finishing up with my mom and the kitchen I went to my room and dialed Nathan's number. I was so excited all the while hoping he would be home and pick up. The sound waves of his voice went straight through my ears to my heart. I couldn't wait to be able to wrap my arms around his neck while he pulls me close to him. I wanted him to hug me like he hasn't seen me in 3 years rather than 3 months.

"Hello?"

"Hey, you. What you up to?" I smiled so big I know he could hear my lips part through the phone.

"Oh, nothing. Wus up?" he seemed withdrawn, but I wasn't worried about that now. I just wanted to see him.

"Well I made it home, so I wanted to see you if you're not busy?" I replied

"Uhhhh, yeah. Yeah, sure we need to talk anyway." He said as if it just crossed his mind.

"Okay, cool. Um, when do you have time to meet? I asked with my curiosity elevated.

"I can see you in about an hour, how's about that?" He suggested

I looked down at my watch. "in an hour? sure" I exclaimed.

"Ok." He paused for a moment as if he didn't expect me to agree. "Well, see ya then."

"ok, Bye." Nate hung up the phone first. He usually waits until I do.

I was nervous about what Nate had to discuss. The tone in his voice was not one of someone that would be bringing me good news. I won't lie and say that I didn't expect obstacles in our distant relationship, I just hope it's not something cliché like *"he found new love"* or something like that. I would be devastated say the least. Whatever is it I know that it will work out Nate and I love each other, and love prevails in all things, right?

Chapter 21 [NATHAN]

"Jesus, how am I gonna tell her?" I said to myself as I laid back on my bed after Denise's call. I knew she was going to try and call me again once she landed and got settled. Truthfully, I've been avoiding her. You see since she's been gone away, I've had time to really think about what I really want to do in my life. My passion is not running track or taking over one of my fathers' businesses. I want my own business doing something that I'm passionate and excited about. After about a month of Denise being gone, I ran into Leah. She had just had her baby a few months earlier and was in the store looking for a formula. She had her hair in a high bun with little make-up. Leah always was good-looking but always seem to be running from something. I don't Denise has called Leah lately to check up on her. She approached where I was stocking pampers, I stood up anticipating a possible awkward greeting.

"Hi Leah, right?" I wanted to make sure she remembered me. We haven't talked too much since our meeting at Denise's house for junior prom.

"Yeah, Nathan?" she said with a little doubt. "Denise's boyfriend?"

"That's right, how are you?"

"Oh, hey as good as I can be ya know, you?" she seemed guarded as if she was trying to put on a face that really wasn't hers.

"Good, can't complain." I walked over to the basket a leaned a little closer. "So, who is this, Leah?"

She pushed a button or two on the car seat that was in the basket and revealed the most handsome baby boy that had the exact dimples of his mother. His hair was curly and believe me it covered every inch of his head. "This is Lewis Jr., say hi, say hi." She said trying to get him to say hi in a cute playful manner.

"Wow Leah, you're a momma." I didn't know what else to say. It's amazing how life goes.

"Yep, a momma." She laughed a little with that same cute smile she had in high school. "At first I was scared out of my mind and felt that I wouldn't be able to be someone else's mother. With my troubled past with my mother being on drugs, her prostituting and in-and-out of foster homes, I just knew I would fail. But once I saw his face," she touched her sons' cheeks with such compassion, "I knew he was a gift from God and with him, I'll change the cycle of failed motherhood and raise my child up with as much love as I can give him. He is my passion now."

"Well, Leah that sounds great. Ya know I know you'll be a great Mom." I emphasized. She smiled a little as if she needed to hear those words. Leah to me was like an angel who mysteriously lost her wings. She always seemed to hide the beauty that she holds on the inside except when she smiled her inner just shine so bright, full of light.

"Thanks, Well I better get going," she said humbly

"Alright, nice seeing you too." I started to walk back to the stack of boxes I was stocking.

"Yeah, you too. Oh! Nathan?"

"Yeah?"

"How's Denise, I haven't heard from her in a while? It's just been crazy I know." She explained

"Oh, she's okay, at Howard studying Psychology." I just gave the basics because I didn't really know the deal between her and Denise, so I'll just let women deal with women.

"Ok, well tell her I said hi and I love her." She said it as if she really missed De-De.

"I sure will Leah," I assured her. She nodded with a smile of gratitude in return and turned and walked away.

She walked back to her previous life before our encounter. I'm sure Leah's Mom had plans for her to go to college, get married, start a family, etc. That story seems to always be the norm and what you run to when you're afraid of doing what you want to do in life and not what your parents will be pleased with. I started thinking of the next chapter of my life. Was it to go to college and study business like my Dad wanted or to pursue my passion in culinary arts? I thought about it throughout the day while at work on what should I do. Should I give up my scholarship to Georgetown and not be near Denise or go and most likely resent Denise because of my regrets. I wasn't sure what I wanted to do but I know I had to decide quick.

Chapter 22 [MARISSA]

James has been calling me nonstop for the past 2 weeks. I'm just starting to get tired of this game he thinks I don't know he is playing. Don't get me wrong I care about James but not enough to be second place. I know my worth enough to know when I'm not a priority. I knew as soon as I mentioned Leah's pregnancy he would get in his feelings and basically tune our whole conversation out or take anything I say concerning Leah as an attack. I'm so over this whole situation with him. Bump it. I'm sure my mother would be rolling over in her grave if she knew I was selling myself short for a guy that is clearly in love with another and cannot move on with the fact that:

"SHE HAS A BABY WITH ANOTHER GUY. IDIOT!!" I screamed as I slammed the door to my room in my dorm.

"What's your problem?" my roommate Angie asked. I didn't see her in the room before I had my outburst. She startled me, to say the least.

"Oh, hey girl. I didn't know you were here. Same ole' same ole'" I fanned a wave and walked over to my bed and threw my bag on flopped down on the bed with my hands behind my head facing the ceiling.

"When will you learn. He is what you call a womanizer. He is using you for the time being until this other chick is available. Let it go girl." She said shaking her head as she turned back to her desk. My roommate was a brutally honest nag, but I liked her. She kept it real, too real. I told her she may need to tone that down if she wants to be a psychologist. Have a little empathy for goodness sake. But she was right, I needed to just end it with James for good. He was so self-absorbed. I thought Lewis was bad but maybe I was mistaken. I was a bit of a manizer during that time with Lewis. Maybe that's why I resent Leah even more.

I sat up a little in the bed leaning on my side to talk to Angie "I brought up the fact that Leah was pregnant and…"

"Girl why you did that?" Angie snapped as she turned to look my way from her computer. "You could have talked about anything but that. Are you still going to see her?"

"Well, I'm thinking about it. Besides me bringing Leah up had nothing to really do with her but it did. I just wanted to see his reaction to the news…then…maybe." I stuttered but of course Angie finished my sentence.

"You'll find out if he still has feelings for her instead of you?" she shook her head.

"Well, yeah!" I flapped my arms up once and landed them on my sides. "wouldn't you want to know?"

"I don't know what I would do, but we're talking about you. Back to reality please." Angie snapped her fingers twice. "Focus."

"Ok." I groaned. "He's been calling me."

"Yes, I know. I'm tired of lying." She got up from her desk to pick up her bag for track practice. "Handle that sister."

She hit the top of my show as she exited the door. "See ya cow."

"Alright."

I laid there thinking of how I got into this situation and why was it so hard for me to let go. I should have never lost my virginity to James. But growing up next door to him it was bound to happen. James was not your typical boy next door, well in my opinion. He was fine-fine. He never started off as an "ugly duckling" that later became the "dashing prince." He never slacked in the looks department I can give him that. James did have a problem with keeping focus on one girl at a time since Leah. I never asked James for anything other than friendship because I already knew his hang-up about Leah, but he can at least ACT like I mean something to him.

I've lived in Hempstead, Tx for as long as I can remember, in the same house with my Mom and Dad until my Dad moved out. Here in Hempstead is either you are a church girl or the latter, well maybe that was just my Dad. He was strict; really strict. He would be outside with his rifle when a boy would come to the end of the driveway. I remember this one time I was outside waiting for the bus. I would sit on the back of my dads' truck eating my breakfast or reading. This day, a new kid from across the street wanted to catch the bus in front of my house instead of walking further down the street where the other kids must catch the bus. You see, my Dad talked to the bus driver and now I'm able to be picked up in front of the house:

"Hey son, what you need?" my dad came out of nowhere and asked the boy.

"Oh, nothing sir. I'm just catching the bus." he tried to say as innocently as possible. He was telling the truth.

"Now, ain't gonna be no courting going on over here son. You hear me?" my Dad seemed to threaten. He was embarrassing the hell out of me over nothing.

"Oh, yes sir. No disrespect Mr. Orville." He said with his hands up a little as to surrender.

"ok, I mean that," Dad said as he walked back toward the house and went in.

I looked at the boy and he gestured as to ask what he did. I mouthed to him "nothing" and shook my head a little as to translate not to worry about him. He never caught the bus there again.

Even though my Dad was strict as he was, he was more relaxed with James. Knowing what I know now my Dad is a bad judge of character. Like father like daughter. Growing up next door to James we've had our spats outside as kids. Seen each other grow up. Seen each when we've been down. So, him being a bully in junior high is due to his parents split, that's when he was just angry at everybody until Leah. She changed something in him, she has a piece of his heart that he's not willing to take back. After Leah and James stop speaking to each other or "broke up," he started to come by my locker more just to say "hi." I felt like he was stalking me so when I saw him outside one day, I decided to confront him and see what his problem was. Never thinking that this day would change how I thought and saw James Dietrich.

"Is it something you need to say? "I asked.

"About?" he sarcastically said. He was always a smart ass. I think he couldn't help himself.

"I don't know but by the way you are staring, something must be on your mind," I said with a skeptical look on my face because he looked at me in a way that I have seen from him before. It was awkward, so I just laughed it off. My friends noticed the same thing "every day I see you spying on me James but I'm sure Leah wouldn't appreciate that now would she?" I had to throw that in there. For God knows how long I had to hear about how "Leah did this, and Leah did that."

"And why would you care what Leah would appreciate or not?" he had this smirk on his face that I wanted to slap off.

"I DON'T." he was such an asshole sometimes. I know he said that just to get me started. But to be honest I don't have any issue with Leah. Were little girls, it's not that serious.

"Well ok, wus up then?" he was so close I thought I was going to fall backward.

"With what?" I said then I thought about it some more. Why would he be so interested in me now? "Oh, I see, you want some ass, don't you?"

"I didn't say that." he was such a liar. But his charming statue is what I couldn't resist.

James and I became involved and have been "hooking up" ever since. We never defined our relationship, but I never felt so distant from him as I do now. He is a familiar face here at PV but I'm sure I'll be fine if I would never see him again. I must let this guy go and move on before I become too tainted.

Chapter 23 [LEAH]

It was nice seeing Marissa at the hospital. I didn't know what to expect. Ever since grade school, Marissa has been a thorn in my side. I'm not sure what the animosity was all about but hopefully it can be settled for once and for all. I had just fed the baby and put him down to sleep when there was a light tap on the door. I got back in the bed and covered a little to be decent.

"Come in, it's open." Marissa walked in with the cutest little bear. It had on a red, blue and white plaid shirt, with little blue khaki shorts and a red bow tie. She smiled and waved a little wave and paused at the door. I signaled for her to come further. "Come one, it's okay." I looked over at Junior to make sure he was still sleeping. She walked over slowly with a look of not pity but of concern and the spirit of making a truce.

"Hey Le-Le," she said

"Hey girl, what'chu been up to?" I asked as we both giggled a little.

"Ohhhh." She said as she sat at the edge of the bed and rolled her eyes in the back of her head in exhaustion. I know who she was dealing with. James can be a handful. "nothing I can't let the Lord handle. How are you and Lewis? I know this has to be shaking his soul right about now."

I laughed. "Girl, so far he's been on top of things you know," I said with a little bit of surprise in my voice. "So right now, we're okay. I'll just let it unfold ya know." I explained looking at my son.

"That's good Leah. No really. I know we've had our differences. To be honest I was, a little jealous of you and James. You see, he was my first and we were not together but together. It was complicated, Leah. Then when you came along, he looked at you in a way I've never seen anyone look at another person before. And I wanted that from him. But I had to realize that wasn't your fault. Sometimes love hits you unexpectedly, but it can also teach you to love yourself in many ways than one. I apologize Leah for my behavior over the years."

I was deeply touched. I've never seen Marissa in this type of space before. I think being with James even though it was a thorny situation, it did help her grow. I'm proud of her. "Oh, come here." I gave Marissa a big hug. We both laughed and smiled. "No apology needed. Love you, Marissa."

"Love you too Leah." Marissa sniffled a little. She reached to the side and picked up the bear. "here give this to Lewis Jr., I hope he likes it."

"I'm sure he will, thanks." I took the bear and cuddled with it a little. I love stuff animals, so this was perfect.

"Well, let me head on back. I got a final to study for and I'm not sure if that's gonna go so well for me." She said with a laugh.

"Oh, ok. I'm glad you stopped by." I said as I sat up a little in the bed to adjust.

"no problem." She paused by the door for a moment then turned to leave.

"Oh, Marissa!"

"Yeah" she turned back around.

"Thanks again. I really appreciate it."

She did the typical Marissa, she winked and walked out the door with her famous sashay. What can I say, I love her? I hope that Denise still feels the same way. I haven't heard from her in a while. Something must be up, or has she just moved on with her life and forgot about me.

Chapter 24 [DENISE]

I borrowed my Mom's car and told her I was going out for a spell and visit Nate. I drove a couple of miles to Nates' parents' house. It was not late but too late to where I want to disturb his parents if they were home. I told Nate to be outside so we could talk elsewhere by the time I would pull up.

I parked on the side of his street next to the tallest bush in the yard. Nathan's area was a little bit nicer than ours but all the same. The people were the same just a different tax bracket. I saw him sitting on the curb when I pulled up. He got up from the curb looking a little bit taller than last I saw him and handsome as usual. He pulled the handle to get in, but it was locked. I didn't realize it, so I jumped a little when he tapped on the window and signaled that it was locked. I unlocked the door and he opened it and got in.

It was like breathing the air that blows off the waves at the beach when he stepped in the car. He was too fresh. I couldn't wait to wrap my arms around him.

"Hey." He said

I hesitated a little. I could feel the awkwardness in the air and my heart was racing. "Hey." We hugged each other. With every breath I took I inhaled his very being. "I missed you."

"missed you too." We finally let go of the lock we had on each other. "Can I kiss you?" he asked holding my chin as if he was inspecting my face.

"Yes."

We kissed very passionately. Too passionately, I stopped Nate because I knew something didn't feel right.

"What's the matter Nathan?" nudging him back from my lips. "I know when something is going on with you."

"I have something to tell you, but I don't know how." He looked confused as he sat back in the passenger seat. "It's not. That I. I've. I've decided not to go to Georgetown." He looked my way with a look of worry and gloom. "Now look De-De..."

"What?" I couldn't believe what I was hearing. "Where did this come from?"

"Look, I had been thinking after I ran into Leah a couple of months ago..." he began

"Ok, whoa, whoa, Leah? What does she have to do with anything? What's going on Nathan?"

Nathan took a deep breath. "She doesn't; it's just that seeing her that day and seeing how her life changed from one decision...and she seems to be ok. So, why can't I be able to do what I really want to do instead of what people expect of me?" he looked at me for understanding but I just couldn't due to the heartache. "Denise say something, please."

"Say what?" I just sat there with a look of disgust I'm sure.

I didn't see in my mind where Nathan and I would survive if he decides to not go to Georgetown. From the looks of it,

He has decided already. That would explain the missed calls and distant conversations on the phone.

"I don't know. just something…" he said

"You know what I think, you decided this weeks ago. You knew each time I called you would have to deal with the guilt of not letting me know or even consider how this affects me. You purposely ignored me. As a matter of fact, you probably had this plan all along Nate. you never had any intention on coming to D.C." I said with tears starting to form in my eyes. He just sat there and let me vent. That's the least he could do.

"I understand you're upset De-De, but we could still make this work." He proclaimed

"How, huh, how?" I put my elbow on the window ledge of the car door and rested my head on my bent arm. "you have no idea."

"I don't know yet, but I'll think of something." He leaned forward to look me in my face for reassurance. There is none.

"Look, Nate, you do what you have to do for your life. I don't want to hold you back from something you want to do. Until you can find a way, let's just take a break. For now. I just can't deal with this right now." I proposed. Regardless if he agreed or not, that was MY decision.

"I don't want that De-De." he side-eyed me.

"Well, I think that's the best decision for me. If it is meant to be, it'll be Nate."

We sat there in the car not saying anything for a few minutes. Nate turned his head and looked at me. I faced him and looked in his eyes for as long as I could. I reached out to grab his hand, but he moved it away, opened the car door and closed it back. I watched as he walked back toward the front door of the house. He opened the door and didn't even look back. The door slammed.

It was over. What I thought was going to be a lifetime was not. Who's to say, it probably was for the best, it probably wasn't but I'm glad that I experienced it thus far. Call it puppy love if you want but everyone starts somewhere in this game. I drove around for a while just thinking how to get over Nathan and it came to me about him talking to Leah. I have been missing her calls, but I have been preoccupied mentally. I guess I can ride by for a visit since I'm out. Hopefully, I don't lose another relationship today.

I still had the address from when she left it on my answering machine. I drove over and found Leah sitting on the porch breastfeeding. The sight of her was something out of a Gerber commercial where they are advising mothers on how breast milk is the best choice for your baby instead of formula. I pulled further into the carport area. She told me that this was Lewis's uncle's old place and he was letting them stay there for the time being. I sat in my care for a minute before getting out. Leah had noticed me driving in and adjusted herself with the baby to stand. I prepared myself to see the friend I haven't been so friendly too. I hoped she would forgive me, and we can start over.

When she recognized it was me, she smiled very sweetly and waved. It was nice to see her face again. I opened the door to get out and on with my life.

Chapter 25 [LEWIS]

"God, I hope Leah cooked." I was just leaving my job at my Dad's company Nichols Construction & Remodeling. We just got this big bid in Houston to remodel a downtown building and I've been working late for the past month. Leah has been very understanding about it all, I don't want my woman nor my kid to want for nothing, so I must do what I got to do. Don't get me wrong it's been a rough road, but I think we're getting the hang of things. If I can get Leah to open and communicate more, everything will be just fine. I hope.

I've enjoyed my time with Leah thus far. She's so beautiful and doesn't know it. Her humbleness is so appealing that my heart just melts every time I see her. I remember in high school when I took a leap of faith and just showed up at her house to take her to school. After dropping her off the night before, the energy was so crazy, she knocked me off my game completely. She was a fantasy to me. Whichever way life goes with her I wanted to be there:

"What are you doing here?" she said. She gave me the look I desired from her and that was of shock and awe. It seemed it took a lot to get this girl's attention and I was determined to.

"I was on my way to school so I figured I'll stop by and catch you before you caught the bus and see if you would like a ride instead." I felt playa but in a good way, not a conniving way.

"Do I have a choice?" she asked in that sarcastic, I'm one step ahead of you anyway. It was a turn on.

Of course, I had to clap back at that, I knew who I was dealing with. I laughed. "You do but, why choose the bus?" I opened the door to the car as to insist for her to get in. "C'mon before we're late." Of course, she stepped into the car reluctantly, but I can change that mood. I got in and took off down the road. "I just wanted to surprise you that's all."

"You have a way of surprising someone that's for sure." She shifted her body in the seat. The jeans she had on hugged every curve of her voluptuous hips and thighs which held up the fattest ass that I've seen. Damn! was all a brother could say.

We pulled up to the street to turn into the student parking lot. I always park away from the crowds because my car got keyed a while back. "We're kind of early," I said.

"Yeah, I usually don't get here this early, riding the bus and all," she said referring to me changing her routine today. She just can't go with the flow.

"Leah, Leah." She made me smile as always.

"What? And why do you always do a little laugh every time I say something. It's kind of annoying?" she asked clearly aggravated.

"I'm annoying you, Leah. Wow!" I teased.

"I'm talking about your behavior, Lewis."

"Well okay, you know what's annoying to me?"

"I'm sure you're going to tell me." she rolled her big beautiful eyes a little.

"That right there. Why must you always give me the cold shoulder? What have I done?"

She unbuckled her seatbelt and turned to face me. I didn't know what she was going to say but I played it cool. I propped my elbow on the window seal of the door waiting on her next response. I already knew what was going to come out of her mouth.

"Lewis, I honestly think you're an overbearing, overhyped, womanizing misogynist. But I shouldn't assume you have such an extensive resume before knowing for myself. So, I guess my "coldness" is me really being "cautious." No offense!" she explained. I must admit it kind of stung to hear her describe me in that manner, but I made light of the situation.

"You really think I'm overhyped?" I said jokingly.

"Out of all the other stuff, I said, 'overhyped' is what you're concerned about, ok?"

We both laughed.

We both got out of the car and walked toward the building. I thought about what Leah said and was not surprised. Rumors are what they are; rumors. People say a lot of things when they get hurt or realize they played themselves. "I admit I like the ladies and it may appear that I have no soul when it comes to the matter of the heart, LEAH..." she laughed at the emphasis of her name, it was cute, "but I do. You'll be surprised how some of these girls do me."

"Yeah right!" she said with a side-eye.

"Seriously, what, you don't think dudes don't get their feelings hurt. Yall can be cold. No offense." I teased. "look how you do me, with your shortness and 'talk to the hand' persona." I tried to imitate her persona, but I think I just made a spectacle of myself, but I didn't mind. I would do anything to see her smile. "I'm just saying though, what's up Leah?" she knew I wanted to get to know her better. Leah is a tough safe to crack but I was determined to pick the lock to her heart.

"Lewis..." she started to respond until she was interrupted by none other than cock-blocking James.

"Hey, Leah?" there he was standing with a few of the brothers on the team. He made sure she noticed him too. Yelling her name like he's marking his territory. I won't take it as disrespect since she's not my lady, yet.

I pulled up to the house and saw her and Denise outside on the porch. I was surprised to see this scene especially since Leah hasn't heard from Denise in a while. Denise was that boogie southern-bell type. She never had an opinion about me and Leah being together from what I know. It didn't really matter but I sure didn't want her to be filling Leah's head with nonsense. I parked my truck and got out after grabbing my other belongings. I can see Leah's smile from the walkway as I approached the porch. Seeing this at the end of the day makes it worth getting up at the crack of dawn. I hope Denise is not staying long, I'm not in the mood for company.

"Hey, what's going on here?" I teased the ladies as they just finished having a good cackling session, I'm sure before I drove up. I kissed Leah on the forehead as sweet as I could being tired and all.

They laughed.

"Nothing, just catching up," Leah said as she looked me over for one of her silent inspections. She's attentive like that. "Junior fell asleep after I fed him, so he should be down long enough so you can get a little rest."

"Alright," I said as I caressed her chin. "So, What's up Denise. I see you do remember your way back home, huh?

She rolled her eyes a bit as to seem annoyed. "Whatever, Lewis. How are you too?"

"Can't complain, busy, but it's all good." I looked down at Leah and kissed her again. "Let me go check on Jr. Did you cook?" I was starving. That's one thing she can do is cook amongst other things.

"Yeah, it's in the oven staying warm. You don't have to heat it up."

"Ok great. Alright Denise, nice seeing you." I waved as I went into the house.

"I can't wait until the house is finished, then we can move up out of here." I thought as I threw my stuff on the bed

and began taking off the dirty work clothes, I had on filled with lord knows what. I didn't tell Leah, but I've been working with my Dad on the home I'm getting built for us. I do own part of a family construction company. I haven't told Leah that part of my life yet as well. All she knows is that I have a job working with my Dad at the family business. She had to take off from her job at the record store to stay home with the baby. She wants to start school soon, which is fine, but she wants to work as well. I'm not about to have that. So, I'm trying to get this house completed before that time so that I can let her know she doesn't have to work. It's going to be like pulling teeth for her to agree because of her pride. She's tough like that but not in a bad way.

I hopped in the shower to wash the stress of the day off before I went to check on my son. I still can't believe it sometimes that I'm a father. I was scared shitless when Leah told me and when I saw the belly it came down on me like a ton of bricks:

"Get yo hands off me. Don't touch me." She said to me with her hand ready to punch me in the face.

I just said the dumbest thing I could say. I messed up this time. "Stop trippin' Leah! What am I supposed to say?" I said with my hands up in anticipation of receiving a Mike Tyson punch. I've never seen her this upset.

She just told me about the pregnancy and showed me her stomach where she was starting to show a little. "NOT ARE YOU GONNA KEEP IT!" she yelled.

We both sat there in silence for a few minutes. She seemed to be deep in thought. I didn't say much either. I wanted to let her cool off a bit. I hate trying to communicate in anger, it reminds me of my mother. I wanted to let Leah know how I truly felt about her so many times, but the fear of her rejection was too much to bear. Regardless of my hang-ups of not being able to connect with Leah I took a chance and told her how I felt.

"Leah. Despite what you may be thinking, I do care and I... I do love...you. I love you." I was nervous. I know she didn't believe a word I said but I didn't care. I'll make her see. "We'll figure this out. I have some money saved up and I already work with my dad for now." I decided not to tell her about my whole situation on how I get money. I took her hand to reassure her. "It's ok, just trust me."

Jr. was sound to sleep. He'll be up in a little over an hour for his next feeding. I went into the kitchen to see what Leah prepared for me. "Yes!" I said out loud with a fist pump. She made sweet cornbread, cabbage with the bacon, just like I like it and meatloaf with brown mushroom gravy. I couldn't wait to dig in.

[WAAHHH]

"Ugh, you got to be kidding me," I said in frustration throwing my head back. I put my plate back in the oven. "C'mon little man, daddy just need five minutes to eat." I walked out of the kitchen to go toward the baby's room.

"Go eat, I got it." Leah zoomed passed me so fast, all I saw was her backside twisting down the hall. "Aww, shhh, shhh now." I heard her tell the baby. She walked back out with our son. It was a beautiful sight to see. "Babe, go eat."

Standing there staring at Leah and Lewis Jr. I must have been in a trance. "Oh, ok you sure? You got it?"

"Yeah" she kissed Jr and continued consoling him. He calmed down a little bit.

"Alright." I gave her a kiss and went to finish my dinner. Days like this seemed too short. It was always the baby this the baby that but, I wouldn't trade it for the world.

Chapter 26 [Nathan]

Things didn't go so well with Denise. I can't believe she broke up with me. I thought that she would at least try and work things out or see it from my side, but I guess that was too much to ask for. After the Thanksgiving break, I tried to call Denise thinking maybe she was just angry that things were not going the way that she planned. She can be very controlling at times. It's either her way or the highway.

RING! RING!

"Hi, You've, reached Denise, I can't come to the phone right now, but if...." I slammed the phone down. This is so unfair. After all, I've been nothing but understanding, patient and loving toward Denise. "Bitch!" I was growing angrier by the day, but I'm will not let Denise take me out of character.

I took a deep breath, grabbed my basketball and headed out the door to the courts. I needed to get Denise in the back of my head. Bad enough my Dad has been giving me the cold shoulder ever since I announced that I wanted to go to culinary school to become a Chef than go to a university. I just want to do what I want to do for a change, not what everybody else expects me to do.

"Dad, can we talk?" I approached my dad after dinner. He is usually relaxed and open to reason. He can be a real asshole if he hasn't eaten.

"Yeah, what's going on son, how are things?" he asked.

My Dad owns an auto repair and parts shop and it's been very successful over the years. My mother was a head chef at a five-star restaurant but decided to stay home to raise me after she got pregnant. My father was a big part of that decision. He's a die-hard Christian. He prays and loves God only but sometimes I believe he doesn't know him. I know I'm only 17 so maybe we both have the same theory so to speak, I just try to channel in the spirit more.

"Dad, I know this is going to not be what you want to hear, but I want to own my own business…"

"Ok?" he interrupted.

"But I'm not talking about the shop, I want to own my own restaurant, so I want to go to culinary school."

"Culinary School?" he said in disbelief that this subject is coming back up after he said it was closed.

"Yes, Dad."

"Culinary School? Why can't you let this go?" he asked putting down his paper he was reading.

"Because it's in my heart. I mean, Mom was a chef." This look came over his face I didn't understand.

"So, who's gonna run the shops when I'm gone?"

"Dad, I understand that. Can I ask you something?" I proclaimed as I tried to think of a way to come off as disrespectful.

"Go 'head." He sighed.

"Would you want me to do something I'm passionate about for the rest of my life or in a way settle for something out of guilt for the rest of my life." That last part scared me because the look on my fathers' eyes felt like I sucked the life out of him. I did get a sense of relief as may be the feeling a flower gets when it grows to its intended creation. My father got up out his chair, looked at me, I stepped back a little. He tossed the paper in the chair seat and walked toward the kitchen. My mother was standing there finishing up the dishes I'm sure listening in.

"Talk to your son." He tilted his head back toward my direction as he commanded my mother in the most flat-toned voice that has preceded out of his mouth.

My mother mouthed to me, "I'll talk to him." That was about three weeks ago to date and my Dad hasn't said but three words to me. My mother and father's relationship have seen some rocky times, but they are still deeply in love and my mother can get my Dad to see if no one could.

I made it to the courts and started to shoot hoops. I thought about my Dad and Denise. I also started to doubt myself. I guess I got it honest from what my Mother tells me. My Dad was so nervous to talk to my mom he was shaking in his seat. Dad still claims the seats were jacked up but mom's version sound more believable.

They met at a Rockets game almost 20 years ago. I believe Dad said when he saw her, she glowed. Whatever that means. He was with my uncle and his best friend to see the Rockets take on the Philadelphia 76ers. My mom is originally from San Diego and my grandfather was in the military, so my Dad traveled a lot. My dad's family finally settled in California, so I guess my mother was welcoming. It was a couple of days after Valentine's Day and it was my uncle's birthday. They were only about 15 or 16 I think but they saved up doing odd jobs ever since the team started in 1967. But that night they got to see my Dad's favorite player. Elvin Hayes. He was the first-round pick and first overall pick in the 1968 NBA draft. I would always watch him with Dad when I could when I was younger before Hayes retired in 1984.

My mother walked down to the area where they were sitting. He turned to his left and saw the most beautiful girl walking toward him.

"Adam, ADAM!"

"What?" I said lightly because I was in a daze. I'm not sure what I felt but I sure as hell can describe it. It felt like the beginning of spring when the cool breeze caresses your face in all the right places and for a moment your burdens are lifted, and you can feel the kiss of the sun's bright smile warming your whole body.

I heard my brother yell me out of my trance, but I was still fixated a bit. She sat right beside me, and I was tossed and kicked out of my square. I felt like I fell back even though I was sitting down. "You alright? What you gonna do stare the girl down?" he laughed looking down the row at me and leaning back.

"Leave him alone." I can count on Kevin to have my back and try not to make me look like a total idiot, unlike my

brother. They both laughed under their breaths though. "So much for holding back, you straight gone man."

"[tsk] Whatever man." I tried to play it cool of course but her scent melted all that ice. I didn't know what to say to her, but I did know I was interested, and I just wanted to know anything. I was fidgeting a lot. I do that when I'm nervous beyond measure. A little time passed; Hayes just went for another rebound.

"Do you mind?" her voice was angelic.

"Oh, sorry, it's just these seats are uncomfortable." I tried to explain the excuse I came up with. She looked at me with a side-eye. She had the WHATEVER look on her face. It was adorable. Her hair was curly and reached down her back. Her lips were full and soft-looking with lip gloss of cotton candy, Or that's what it looked like to me. She had the biggest dark eyes I've seen, and they sparkled with every touch of light. Her cheekbones were high, holding the cutest chiseled nose. All this beauty was covered in the smoothest dark chocolate skin I've seen in my life. She was God-like. "Sooo I don't run into too many females into sports." I was so nervous. That's was the lamest line ever.

"Maybe because you're running." She responded sweetly. I know she was just being nice by entertaining my pathetic approach at starting a conversation. Either way her response had me intrigued.

Chapter 27 [NATHAN]

After shooting hoops for about an hour, I decided to take a rest on the bench on the side of the court. I felt a little better but still wishing that all these emotions would just fade away. I felt a tap on my shoulder. I turned around and lifted my hand to block the sun from my eyes so I can see who it was. To my surprise, she stood there beautiful as always. I recognized the face but didn't know the name. I've seen her around the neighborhood and said an occasional hello from time to time but not a formal introduction has presented itself. Today may the day for introductions.

"Oh, hey."

"Hello. I thought that was you." She said

"Uh, yeah um I'm sorry we've never...."

"Marissa, Marissa Orville." She held her hand out to shake mine. I looked down and took her hand. This was my first time looking into her eyes. They were mesmerizing.

"Nathan." My mouth was still open.

"I gave you my last name, Mr. Nathan." She suggested and I'm dumbfounded as usual.

"Oh, I'm sorry um…Carter, yeah. Nathan Carter. Sorry about that, I didn't expect to see anyone here." She let go of my hand and smiled. Maybe it was her smile instead of the sun that was in my eyes.

"Well, maybe you should raise your expectations. Of yourself I mean." She added with a soft laugh. "May I sit?"

"Sure, go right ahead." I stood and gestured for her to sit as I was taught. She sat down. I noticed her hips and how her skirt was making sure they stayed in their assigned place. I wish I was her skirt. "So, you back here visiting?"

"Yeah, I decided to take another day before I went back. Needed to relieve some stress, a reminder of me, ya know." She said

"Yeah, I can relate." I thought about my issues with my Dad and my insecurity from the guilt I feel for not wanting to do what my father wanted. I've always wanted my Dad to be proud of me and this decision makes that a distant star to wish upon.

"Ready for graduation?" she asked as she gave me a light nudge. She always has a smile on her face. Her cool, calm and collected persona was a turn on.

"As ready as I'm gonna be. I decided to go to culinary school, I got some backlash from my dad but oh well. I gotta do what I gotta do." I shared it with her. It was easy to talk to her. I hope I didn't say too much. I didn't want to appear weird.

"That's interesting, I wouldn't take you as a chef." She said 'chef' not 'cook' like my dad called it.

"Yeah, my mom was a chef, so I guess I just caught the bug." I laughed a little.

We sat there for about another hour or so and talked. The more I talked to Marissa I realized we had more in common than Denise and me. Don't get me wrong I love Denise it was just nice to have someone that really understood me and to add not at all bad to look at.

"Well, I better get going. I got an early flight tomorrow morning and I haven't started packing. Do you need a ride? I have my Mom's car?" she offered.

"Uh, sure if it's not too much trouble? I'm not that far."

"Oh no problem, let's go." Marissa gestured for me to come on while she shuffled through the keys to finding the right one. I didn't want to walk the two miles back to the house. She unlocked the door starting with mine. A '75 Buick Electra 225, even though it was about ten years old the burgundy paint was still intact. It was clean. I got in and she started the car.

"You know how to operate this baby?" I teased.

She looked at me with her sexy eyes and a slight grin. "Trust, I had my practice." She turned the wheel and whipped out of the parking lot. "This was a gift from my granddad to my dad when I was about nine or ten years old. I used to play like I was driving while he holds me in his lap. "By the look on her face I can tell her thoughts went somewhere else.

"it's a nice ride," I said as I looked around and toward the back checking out the interior.

"Thanks."

Chapter 28 [MARISSA]

I need love, care, and validation, I'll be the first to say it. Who doesn't? Many people have done the unspeakable for it. I love to be loved, I love to be cared for and then to have someone stop in their tracks because the sight of me. It feels good. Don't get me wrong I return the gestures. I love to love and to care and validate as well. I believe it's a double dose of fun. The game of love can be confusing to me at times because of my non-conforming personality. I decided to take an extra day over Thanksgiving break and of course nothing can go the way it's supposed to go in my life. All I wanted to do was take a breather from the emotional roller coaster I've been on with James. I finally decided to really let go and move on and do me. He tried calling my parents, but I didn't take the call.

Now here I am on top of this guy in the front seat making out in my mom's car. Maybe everyone's right, I'm such a slut. But am I?

"Nathan wait, wait."

"What's the matter?" he asked still breathing heavy from the lip lock he just had on me. Damn. He still was rubbing my back and looking at me like he was wanted to devour me.

I moved back to the driver side of the seat. "I really don't know you. I mean. I know you've heard things about me but…" I hesitated.

"No, I wasn't, I wasn't. That didn't cross my mind, ya know, to think you were like that." He looked confused and so was I.

I've always gotten teased for my big legs, butt. I developed very early on and it was hard to get people to see you for who you are and not what they perceive you as just because you look a certain way. Race is one thing; gender is another but there is nothing like body shaming. I've had self-image issues ever since I started my menstrual at the age of nine and a half. It was during the summer and I had just started Vacation Bible School:

I love vampire movies and I was watching this movie on the television that my mom just got. These were during the good times when my mom wasn't arguing and fighting with my dad. It may have been temporary, but I appreciated it while it lasted. I didn't see the title because I caught it in the middle of it. I came in on the part where this guy is trying to research how to kill the vampire that killed his wife. Then there was a black woman in the movie that played "Brandy." I remember her from the re-runs of a television show "Barney Miller".

I started to feel a little discomfort in my underwear, so I decided to go to the bathroom. I got up from the bench that was at the edge of my bed and walked down the hall to the bathroom. As soon as I opened the door, I felt that "wet" feeling. I immediately closed the door and pulled down my underwear and I thought I had been bitten by that damn vampire on the TV down there. I screamed.

"Ahhhhhhh!" It was so much blood. Or so I thought it was, I had never experienced that and what am I supposed to think at nine years old. From my understanding, I had a few more years until that happened. My mom came running in the bathroom.

"What, what?" the bathroom door flew open. She stood there short in statue but thin her hair in a bun. We were the spitting image of each other. "Oh, my Lord. Okay honey, just take them off and I'll get you a pad." She closed the door and then yelled "Turn the shower on!"

I turned the shower on and took off the rest of my clothes and got in. I didn't know how to feel; all I know I was not thrilled. I've heard my mom talk with her girlfriends about being a "woman", but this was for the birds. I cleaned as much as I could until my mom came back in. "You not finished yet? Marissa, it's not as bad as you think, okay."

"I won't it off of me." I griped.

"I've never seen someone so pissed off about becoming a woman." She laughed from a healthy place. I loved to see my mom's smile, it just lit up the whole room. On the contrary, my face must have been a mess. "You get more wrinkles from frowning about it."

I didn't care! I was not ready for this and the changes that were to come with a developing body. And boys came along with it and I was tired of being viewed as an automatic invitation for sexual desire for which were not my own. My adornments are not the surface that defines my purpose, I'm much more. In that moment with Nathan,

I realized this and decided to open my heart and express what I'm feeling. What was the harm?

"Nathan, James was my first and my only. But since then it has been going around that I... ya know…"

"You don't have to say." He put his hand up and smiled. "You're not my first."

"Well, that sums that up," I said nervously. The more I look at Nathan he had a laid-back behavior that keeps you on your toes in the weirdest way. You let your guard down and he'll snatch your heart quicker than the trick of a snake. I liked it. "Thanks for being honest."

"No problem, same to you. Now. Can we talk about what's really bothering you? He asked and leaned back in the car seat.

"I just believed in the cliché of James rather than seeing it for what it really was. It was the typical boy next door romance built off one common thing and not many. They say that's all it takes but I disagree. The heart wants, what the heart wants." I summed it up the best way I could.

"yeah, and then the heart sometimes is not always right." He added. He sat on the other side of the car just as cool, calm and collected. It was different and refreshing. He had a way of telling you what you needed to hear and not what you want to hear, but very sweetly. It was different, so it made me uncomfortable.

"Well, I guess. It was nice seeing you again. I paused. I just thought that I finally know his name now after the many

HIs & BYEs between us without even saying a word.
"Nathan." I smiled an uncomfortable smile.

"Well, alright. I think that was my cue." he laughed a little.
It wasn't like that, but I tend to say things in a way that can
be misconstrued. "Thanks for the ride, to my house that is,"
his smile was big and bright as the sun at high noon on a
spring day in the month of May.

He made me smile. We both laughed. He opened the car
door and stepped out. His style had gripped my interest and
held on tight. I had hoped he said just one more thing
before he left but, that was not going to happen. He closed
the door and began to walk toward his driveway. I started
the car.

[knock][knock]

I thought something was wrong with the car but when I
looked up Nathan was in front of the car knocking on the
hood with a little smirk cross his face. I wasn't sure what
this was about. I rolled down the window on my side.

"Yeah!? Something wrong?" I asked

"You wanna go out?"

Chapter 29 [LEAH]

"LEWIS!!!! OH. MY. GOD. Why? H-H-How? WHEN!?

I could not believe Lewis. Once again, the element of surprise is his specialty. No matter what he does he has to make your life flash before your eyes and just be in a whirlwind of dreams. Good or bad. Over these past two years, Lewis and I have had our trials adjusting. Each of us had our faults and our insecurities were tested and destroyed but through it all Lewis's loyalty has been true. Now I'm speechless, all of what I knew about him has just been erased and I know that a brand-new life is ahead.

I had just had the blindfolds taken off me seconds ago before I was able to behold the most beautiful home I've seen. To hear Lewis, say:

"All for you." I almost passed out. He came home earlier that day around 4:30p. I was surprised to see him when he walked through the door.

"Hey, babe."

I turned around with Jr. running trying to get ahold of and examine something he got off the floor. I was in the middle of cleaning up once again before Lewis usually gets home. I must have a clean house. I think I used it as a mechanism to cope with how I grew up and never shook it. It came in handy though. Lewis didn't look like he had been to work though so I was skeptical. "Hey! Early day?"

"Yeah, we finally finished that project I was telling you about." He stood at the door as if he was waiting for an invite.

"o-kay, are you going to come in and get settled?" I asked as a gesture to his strange behavior. "And that's good, maybe you can get some rest now." I walked toward the kitchen to put away the basket full of laundry I just completed.

"Take a ride with me. I have a surprise for you." Lewis had followed me in the kitchen. He took the basket out of my hand and placed it on the floor. "My aunt said she'll look after Jr. until we get back."

"We can't take the baby, why?" I asked. I didn't mind but I'm not the type to just have other people taking care of my child unless it's an emergency.

"Leah, it'll be alright, c'mon. I'll pack Junior's bag while you get ready." Lewis can be overbearing sometimes in my opinion.

I stood there while he walked down the hall to Junior's room. He swooped him up in his arms as my sweet son ran to him. Lewis loves his son so much. In the beginning, I can remember Lewis having a breakdown about becoming a father so young. It really took him to a different place. But through perseverance and prayer he was able to get the hang of it. We both need more work on ourselves and dealing with raising little Lewis. The progress that we've made so far has shown that it does get better, but I know there would be more stormy days ahead.

I went and took a shower and got ready. It did feel good to have at least an hour to myself without the baby. These days I cherished the comfort of Lewis being here to help on occasion when he is not working. I blow-dried my hair quickly and styled my hair in two big cornrows on both sides with golden clips down the braids. Cleaned up my edges and threw on my sundress, with all the fixings of course. I came down the hall putting on my earring and Lewis and Junior were already in the living room playing around.

"Ok, I'm ready." I interrupted.

"Lovely." Lewis stood there with that same smile he had the day I met him. His words felt like warm butter, the way I melted. Now I began to wonder what he was up to.

I smiled, thank you, "You got the bag out here?"

"Yeah, babe. Right there." He pointed toward the couch. I went over and looked over everything, just to double-check. "We got everything babe, let go please."

"Alright, I'm just double-checking," I explained. We gathered everything and we walked out the house to the truck. Lewis put everything in the back while I put Junior in the middle. Lewis came around to my side of the tuck with a scarf. "Uhm What's that for?" Now it was getting weird.

Lewis laughed. "I knew you were gonna be paranoid." He laughed some more. "It's part of the surprise, Leah. I don't want you to see where we're going."

"Oh, so you can throw me in a ditch somewhere, no thank you." I waved my hands and gave him a dramatic side-eye.

"Leah." He leaned on the seat. "I PROMISE you; you have nothing to worry about. I will never hurt you under no circumstances. I love you, you're the love of my life."

I took a deep breath because the confidence in his words seemed to strike a nerve. I took a deep breath. "Lewis if some…"

"Never." He just looked at me in my eyes.

"Okay, but if I start to feel uncomf…."

"Take 'em off." He interrupted again. "I love you."

I let him place the blindfold over my eyes. I must admit it was scary at first. I heard Lewis close the truck door and jumped a little. I had to calm down. I didn't want him to think I was weird. I just have a problem with being in dark places or maybe it's the control of not being able to see. Nonetheless, the trip was a pleasant one. WE laughed and talked the whole way. He made me feel comfortable at ease, which is something I haven't felt in a long time. The next thing you know I'm finally stepping out of the truck with the help of Lewis and I couldn't believe my eyes.

Chapter 30 [JAMES]

These past two years, thinking on it today, seem to have flown by. Moving to the new dorms they recently built has made it a better experience this year as a junior. I found a tree that had some good shade for me to just take a break before my next class. I've been up late studying for finals and every opportunity I get I dedicated to sleep. Basketball practices seem to be getting longer, I just need a break.

I leaned back on the tree with my bag as a pillow and put m towel over my face. I was immediately in dreamland. I'm not sure how long I was asleep, but I was awakened by a familiar laugh.

"Ha, ha-ha. too funny." She giggled. I lifted my towel from off the top of my head that I was keeping the sun out of my eyes while I catch some eye. She was laughing so much it made me a little jealous. I've never seen her smile so much. "Where did you hear that?" They both sat down at a nearby bench continuing their conversation. I tried to hear as much as I could but was unable to without looking like a stalker. For the past two years, I had to witness the development of a relationship between Marissa and Nathan. Don't get me wrong its water under the bridge but I don't want it thrown in my face each time he comes to visit her. Marissa and I parted ways with a little animosity I believe but not on my part. I'm glad she has moved on. But it does bother me a little because of the way she handled me.

"Oh, so where have you been?" I asked Marissa. She stood in front of me in the middle of the student hall with the most

unbothered face I've ever seen. She is very nonchalant in her approach to conversation anyway, but this was different.

"On break."

"Umm what break, it's after New Year's Marissa?" I advised her.

"My break, James. And why are you asking, you know what don't answer that." She put her palm off and began to walk off. I quickly stepped in front of her to keep her from walking away.

"Hold up, wait. You not gonna just handle me like that. You know good and doggone well I've been calling you, now you tell me who's playing games now." He snapped back.

"YOU, JAMES!!" everyone stopped and looked toward her outburst. I took heed and went to corner in the library to avoid the glaring eyes.

"You see, this is what I'm talking about."

"And what is that, James."

"If things don't go your way you throw a fit like somebody owes you something."

"oh, oh okay James." She began to walk away and then turned back around. "You know what James, not one time you've considered how I feel in this whole situation, not even a sorry." She had her finger up as if she was chastising me like a child. "You've used me, lied to me and

led me on. You were my first and you had the one chance to do the right thing with love, but you made your choice to not take it. So, James, this merry-go-round you keep playing on with me has stopped because I've jumped off. I still love me more than you ever will. Good-bye!" A tear fell from her eye as she turned to walk away.

"Marissa, wait!"

Her words seem to peel the invisible layers of my soul. I've never felt so convicted of my actions. I did mess around on Marissa and then have feelings secretly for Leah as more than just a friend. I tried calling out to her, but she kept going. That was the last conversation I had with her. I would see her around campus here and there. Usually she'll look up at me and just keep it moving. You swear she acts as if we've never seen each other naked.

Gazing upon Marissa still gives me delight in my heart. Her smile is still breathtaking, and I will always remember our time together no matter how dysfunctional. Right now, it's time to do me and I plan on doing me right.

Chapter 31 [DENISE]

"Shhhh-SHIT."

This time we didn't make it to the bedroom before being all over each other. My professor was twenty years or more my senior, but I didn't care. He was fine. I knew I could risk getting kicked out of school, but we were always careful.

"Zed, my leg," I said still breathing from the intense passion. It's been a while since I came to visit him with our schedules being out of sync. As soon as I walked into his apartment, he ripped my clothes off. It's been about a month or so since we last "saw" each other.

"Oh, my bad. You alright?" he asked sounding like he just ran a marathon as he rolled on his back.

"Yeah. You nearly drove a hole in me." I hit him on his thigh lightly.

"Yeah, that was the point." He laughed

"Shut-up." I got out the bed to head to the bathroom, but Zedekiah pulled me back and bit me on my shoulder playing around.

"Ow, Stop!" I pushed him away laughing and headed back toward the bathroom. Zed was fun to be around. I think because he may be going through a mid-life crisis is the reason why he would want to be dealing with someone my age. I didn't care I just wanted to keep my grade and a few extra dollars in my pocket. I wasn't doing so well in my classes because I had decided to change my major to Civil Engineering. Now I'm thinking that I should have never come to Howard. Today was one of those days where I didn't want to really do too much and needed to relax. So, Zed provided that. There was no commitment, no strings attached. For the past couple of years, I've been avoiding relationships. I just didn't have the time or energy. I decided to bury my feelings concerning love deep in the valleys of my heart. I still enjoyed the occasional date here or there but nothing serious.

I met Zedekiah in my sophomore year but not at Howard. I was out and about with my roommate and friend Michelle; she was from D.C. We headed out on a warm spring night just to hang out, take in the night air, take in the murals of the area. Michelle was an artist and she loved to take pictures of the city. We were walking toward 18th and U street when he walked up and stood on my right side. I didn't see him in his entirety I just got a whiff of his cologne. I turned to my right to follow the trail and was able to gaze upon the sexiest man that I have seen since being here.

"Hello."

My heart raced not in a way as to be smitten but raced with pure lust. I started to say something, but the light changed and began to walk with the crowd. "C'mon!" my roommate grabbed my hand to make me move a little faster since I was still fixated on the real-life mural of a man I just saw. As I looked back, he smiled ever so sweetly examining me up and down. At the next light he stopped to crossover to the right side of the street and that was the last, I saw of him.

A couple of weeks go by and what do you know, there he was again. I sat up from the reading position I was on the campus lawn under one of my favorite trees. He was talking to another student I have seen in the dorms. She was throwing herself at him so much I felt embarrassed her or maybe him. He walked away down the walkway toward where I was sitting. All I was thinking was I hope he did not recognize me. The sun was out but not enough to be blinded by it and the wind blew creating what seemed like a conversation between the leaves. As I pretended to read my book and watch him at the same time my eyes locked with his unexpectedly. I did not notice in my transition between watching and "reading" he had already stopped and looked toward my way with that smile he had before.

"I'm sorry, but have I seen you before?" he asked walking onto the grass now where I was sitting.

"Umm, no. I don't think so." I lied.

He took his right hand out of his pants pocket and pointed. "18th and U street. I said hello to you, but I believe you had other pressing obligations."

"Okay, I believe I do recall the day. So, what are you doing here?" I was curious.

"I'm a professor part-time here in the science department. What is your major?" he was very direct. He had this "let's not beat around the bush" approach. I like that, I'm not one for small talk.

"Engineering. Civil to be specific." I replied

"Oh, so I might have you in my class this year?" he suggested

"Maybe, who's to say, well sorry about the, hello but I must say goodbye. I have a class." I got up from where I was sitting and gathered my belongings. He was still standing there watching. I looked toward his way and gave an uncomfortable smirk.

"Zed, you can call me Zed." He said out loud

I turned around. "What is that short for?"

"Zedekiah, but I.." he began

"The last king of Judah."

He turned his head to the right side and bit his bottom lip and just stared at me. I turned and walked away not knowing did I defend him or offended him.

"You gotta go now?" Zedekiah asked

I stuck my head out of the bathroom with my toothbrush in my mouth. "Yea!" I muffled out. He knew the rules no staying over. We've already gone thirty minutes too long of pillow talk as it is. When I said I was so over relationships I meant it. It's funny when Leah and I were younger I was the one everybody saw with the husband, kids, big house and a dog. I guess the roles reversed.

"I have to take care of some business back home with my family and get ready for this summer internship coming up.

You know how important this is to me Zed, so I have to keep with my plan." I finished brushing my teeth and freshening. I put on my jeans and top and sat on the bed to put on my shoes.

Zed sighed and crawled up behind me and kissed me on my neck. I mentally turned off any emotion he was desperately trying to make me feel. "I understand. Alright?"

"Okay???" I know I had this confused on my face, but I kept putting on my shoes. I got up from the bed and looked myself over in the mirror. "Well, I'll call you later, alright?"

Zed laughed a little and leaned back on the bed. "Alright." I knew what he was up to and I didn't want to go there with him. I mean c'mon. What would he want from me other than babies or just sex? He says he doesn't have a wife or kids but I'm not that young to think not. Everything Zedekiah tells me is a lie. I don't want to know; I don't care to know.

I shook my head and headed out the bedroom and toward the front door. The next thing I heard pissed me off because of the petty manner it was done. "About that call later, Denise…that probably won't be alright."

"Understood. It was great, the little time it lasted, Zedekiah." I walked out the door feeling relieved that I dodged that bullet.

Chapter 32 [LEWIS]

I hated the term "playa" to be honest. It sounded like a disease or disorder. I would say lover, but love has been so tainted, I didn't like that title either. I wish that the feeling of wanting to express to someone how much you desire or love them wasn't seen as a disorder for me. If God allowed it why should it be labeled. I can't help the way I love women, but something changed when I saw Leah. When I saw her, I felt like being in a jazz café in an urban town having dinner under deem candlelight. She was sent from heaven and my understanding of love started to grow into the seed she planted in my heart. Each day more beautiful than the next day.

After finding out I was going to be a father, it sent me in a whirlwind of fears and doubts. I thought I was going to pass out, but I kept my cool for Leah's sake. I'll never forget the night I told my Dad. I thought he was going to hit the roof.

"Dad, can I talk to you in your office?" I rubbed my chin trying to think of the words to explain the situation I've created for myself. It was the weekend when my Dad usually is at home when he's not on a project or managing other properties out of state.

"Yeah son, yeah c'mon." My dad limped a little because of the accident he had on a rig about eighteen years ago. He said I had just turned one. He sat in his chair and turned to face the opening of his desk to write. "What's on your mind, Lewis? Nobody's pregnant huh?" he said with a

laugh until he realized I wasn't. "Lewis." His laughter disappeared. He lifted both his arms and flopped them back down on his desk and leaned back in his chair. "You got to be kidding me, son. You got to be kidding me?!"

I sat up in the chair across from my dad with my elbows on my knees. "Dad trust me. I did what I was supposed to but the condom broke."

"THEN YOU PULL OUT!" he yelled.

"I...I... I tried but..." I didn't know what to say. What? Tell my dad the pussy was too good I couldn't let the feeling go. I knew something felt off, but I thought it was just that good.

"Son, don't. Just don't." he stood up and rubbed his chin and started to pace slowly.

"Dad, before you start thinking, Leah is different it's not like..." I tried to explain. I wanted to tell my Dad I loved Leah, but I wasn't in the mood for one of those "you're too young to know" speeches.

"Do her parents know?" he asked

"Yeah." I didn't know what to say. I loved Leah and I was going to be there for her. It really didn't matter what my Dad said I was going to do just that.

"Well, let me get with the girls' parents first and then we'll see what we can come up with. Let me be to process this." He sat back down in his chair with a look of disappointment, but I knew he'll be alright. As much as he

puts on the idea of him being a grandfather delights his heart. That is something he and Mom used to talk about before she passed about three years ago.

"Alright." I stood up to leave. "oh yeah Dad?"

"Yeah son." He said with a sigh.

"I know you think I'm too young and I may not have a clue of what's to come but I do know you and Mom taught me about love. I love Leah Dad, just to let you know."

Chapter 33 [LEWIS]

Leah and I were having our first fight in the house. It's been a year and I know her patience is wearing thin on making it official. I can't blame her, but I just want things to work in its due time. I love her but with all that's been going on and the baby and moving, I just wanted some time to relax and settle before taking on another step in our lives. She was not trying to hear that. Her insecurities and let downs once again were surfacing.

"What do you want me to do Leah? Hmm.? I've done everything you've asked me to do. Is it too much to ask for you to put your trust in me?" I begged.

"Trust you? Then who was she? How did she get this number?" she demanded.

"For the hundredth time, her Mom works for my Dad and sometimes she fills in for her mom. She's been there forever, dang." I said in frustration.

She walked away out of our room and toward the kitchen. Leah was not good at expressing her feelings. So, she takes the smallest thing and blows it up to release her emotion. She likes to turn a mole into a mountain. She's been like this since high school and I know how to get her to trust me more. I took some time to go check on Leah. I can understand her being triggered by another female calling the house asking for me, especially with my past reputation. You live and you learn. I walked into the kitchen and there she was with junior washing vegetables and storing them. She's developed a green thumb and pretty good at it too.

I put my arms around her waist and kissed her neck. "What's the matter?"

She took a heavy sigh. "I'm pregnant."

My eyes widened. I wasn't in a panic like I was the last time. Don't get me wrong the idea of another child will be harder. Lewis Jr is already three, so I know she is feeling the pressure from her mother. I've talked to her mother concerning marrying Leah, but she seems to think Leah is not ready. I didn't really believe that Leah could not, not be ready. We just don't have a piece of paper.

[TRACEY]

Hi, my name is Tracey Bond and I love music. It makes me feel alive, set apart, free. Even when I'm not, the vibrations through my heart to my mind with the words it can bring with a beat of the drum it takes me back to an ancestral plain that I don't want to come back from. Maybe it's because my mother listened to a lot of it while being pregnant with me. I also like to write. It's a release that I can't get enough of. It's my therapy, my cleansing, a chance to start over with each chapter. What do I know about love o be honest; sometimes I don't even love myself. This is the hardship that I go through due to the trials of my parents and their parent before them. Anyway, I met Leah while she was out in her garden. I've been helping her lately and I know her husband/boyfriend or whatever he is, needs to marry her. I can't believe he hasn't noticed her new "crop" growing. What can I say, I get it from my mama?

Chapter 34 [NATE formerly known as Nathan]

God can give you a gift, you lose it then he gives you an even better one hoping you cherish this one better than the last time. That's how it feels to spend time with Marissa. We started dating more and more a couple of years ago. I try to juggle school and visiting her and working and everything seems to be ironing out well. I just finished culinary school and rushed to get Marissa. I would usually come and get her each weekend if my schedule allowed and bring her back home from school. She has been a delight. Marissa just needed someone to listen to her. She made it her business to know everything about me but when it came time for her, she immediately became guarded. We were parked in front of a lake not too far from where we lived. The radio was playing in the background. I wanted to spend more time with Marissa alone before I started my internship. Once again life is getting in the way of a relationship, but I believe it may turn out differently.

Our make-out session was interrupted by a noise outside of the car. Marissa was startled. "What was that Nate?" Marissa never called me Nathan. It's just the way she said it made me feel so comfortable with her. With every movement of her body, her speech the look she gives you when you're telling her about your day as if you're the only living thing on earth, you can feel the love she has trapped inside her screaming to be set free.

"What?" I looked around outside the car. I didn't see anything, and I wasn't interested either. Marissa was looking and smelling so good I was in trance. I still had my hands all over her.

"I thought I heard something; you know how these raccoons are out here." She laughed "I will leave you by yourself, I. Do. Not. Like. Raccoons, Nate."

I laughed a little. Marissa had this way of saying things that would put a smile on your face at any given time. "You would leave me, that's messed up?" I said smiling directly in her face. She grabbed my face with both of her hands and brought me in closer until our foreheads touched. She kissed me with the softest lips. They felt as though they melted as she pressed them against mine. I was in total love with Marissa, I admit, I'm a hopeless romantic. I love being loved and I love to love. There is a stigma about guys like me. I've never fallen into the understanding of the "playa" role. I'm a relationship type of guy. I like women.

"You know I wouldn't. But you better not be too far behind." She laughed and she threw her head back. I kissed her on her neck.

"Ha-ha! Whatever." I teased. "You excited about next year?" I asked knowing she was thrilled.

"Yeah, I guess." She said with a big smile. She tried to hide it, but it wasn't working. Marissa decided to transfer to TSU for their nursing program. Which means she would be closer to me working as an intern at Brennan's. I was happy about it too. The distance that was between us before was not long but then it was.

"Uh-huh? You know you're excited." I teased. "I am too. I enjoy being with you." I rubbed the top of her forehead.

"Stop, you are making me feel stuff." She blushed and buried her head in my shoulder.

"Girl you crazy." I laughed and just held her.

Chapter 35 [MARISSA]

What's promised to me? Love. It says so in the good book. You must do some work because love is a lot of things. Love is in every aspect of life. The beginning, the middle and the end. Without love, what is your purpose? We all look for love whether it's in another person, a hobby, food, faith; love is the driving force that keeps this thing called life together and I intend to grab it each time it comes my way. Love won't harm me. Well, it has before but everything turned out fine. My time with Nate these past two and a half years have been wonderful. We just understand each other. I must admit I was guarded, really guarded. I didn't trust him just because he was male. When I approached him a couple of years back, I was mad, upset and pissed off. SO, I did intend on just using him for a moment but then I realized the same behavior that I allowed people to do to me I was planning on doing it to him. How hypocritical of me. I thought, quickly remove yourself from this situation, Marissa, so I chose to embrace him and the way he loves is breathtaking.

It was nice to be able to transfer to TSU next year. For one, I wouldn't be under the watchful cloud of James. It seems that since I called it quits with him, I see him everywhere or mainly during the times Nate would come to visit me when I'm not able to come home for the weekend. His whole presence just got on my nerves. How am I supposed to get over the hurt he caused me if I must be reminded with each bypassing moment on any given day? The agony. So once again here we are walking in opposite directions, but an invisible string keeps tugging at me. I tried to keep walking and ignore him but he's too proud for that.

"Marissa." He stepped in front of me stopping my stride. I nearly fell over him. Same James from high school by any means necessary he will get your attention. It's all about him.

"What James? I have things to do. I don't have time..."

"Can I just say this to you, and I'll let you be on your way." He pleaded.

I stood there looking past him with my hand on one hip. I blurted out, "Go 'head!" I was so angry. I thought I was better, but I was still angry at James for how he used or better yet how I allowed him to use me.

James had a look of intimidation on his face before he began to speak. I can imagine the image of me was something he was not used to. "In life, you take chances to be ultimately happy and find love, and I want to thank you for taking that chance on me. I didn't deserve it. I've been taught to never let my guard down and with that I misjudged you. I'm sorry. I glad that you're happy and I wish you the best."

I've never heard James say anything like this. It was nice to hear him say he's sorry. I could feel my face softening, just a little, to accept his act of kindness. "Well, thank you, James. I appreciate that and I wish you the best." I continued to walk past James on my way to start packing for my move to Houston. This was a new chapter for me in my life and James was not going to be a part of it. I will not allow anyone to come into my life to play games and bring drama. Yes, I have baggage too, but I know I'm an honest person and this you will know upfront. I intend on living my life stress-free and being with Nate has been the happiest time in my life.

Chapter 36 [LEAH]

"...sustainable love even when tainted.

With Love, Lewis"

He said he would never do it again. He said he loves me. He said that he will get help. He said I was the most precious thing to him. Then tell me. Why am I sitting here in this grand house, with all these grand things with a busted lip and bruised face? My eye was nearly closed shut from the blows that Lewis gave me the night before. I'm not sure what has gotten into him lately. First it started off with talking to me in a manner that he has never done. Then it went to grabbing, then pushing to finally full blows to my body. I'm not sure what is it that I do to tick him off. I try to do everything he asks.

We got married before the twins were born prematurely. We ended up having girls and they are so beautiful; they look just like Lewis. I can understand the stress he's under having three kids and a wife to take care of but what does that have to do with my face being connected to his fist I can't understand. I told him there will not be a next time ever again. I threatened to leave him in the past and never did but I can't take this anymore. I must think of my safety and the safety of my children. I don't want to be like my mother being beaten up every night by some man who keeps saying all the things you want to hear but never follow it up with action.

I tore the letter up that Lewis left me the next morning. I don't need another apology letter or flowers or any other material things that he may feel can mask the true monster that he is becoming or maybe was from the start. I went and checked on the twins they were down for their nap and Lewis Jr was at preschool for half the day. I grabbed the baby monitor and headed out in the back yard for some R & R to sort things out as to what will be my next step to flee from Lewis. I sat on the back steps and bowed my head in my hands.

Dear God,

I come to you today in need of direction and forgiveness. You are the maker of everything good and perfect and I do believe this marriage is not what you want for me nor my children.
Lord guide me in the direction you want my life to go. Guide me in your path of righteousness for your namesake. I am weary and heavily burden and I beg of you lord, please remove this burden from my heart. Fill me with gladness and your joy once again so that I may know that it is you father who is with me. In Jesus name.
Amen.

When I lifted my head, Tracey was standing with garden tools at the edge of the steps.

"You alright?"

I sniffled a little and wiped my face. "Yeah." I'm usually embarrassed for anyone to see what I'm really going thru with Lewis but today I was fed up and I didn't care.

"Oh. My. God. What happened to your face?" Tracey lifted my face by my chin and examined it.

"It's nothing, Trace…" I tried to change the subject but of course, by the look of my face I couldn't get out of this one. I've been making up explanations to Tracey for some time now. I bumped into the side of the table; I was out playing with Junior that type of thing. I told Lewis about Tracey questioning the abuse. All he would say is. *"It's not anyone's business, got it?"* Of course, like a dummy I would back down and 'fall back in line.'

"The hell it is. He's beating you too?" Tracey got loud

"Can you lower your voice, and what do you mean too?" I asked knowing good and well what Tracey was referring to.

"Don't play dumb Leah, cause you're not. You know good and damn well he's messing with that hussy where he works. She done already got bold enough to call your house." Tracey held no punches. It was nice to have someone tell it like it is for a change.

"His house you mean," I added.

Tracey came and sat next to me on the steps. "You have to get out of this situation Leah. Do it for your children? They can't be in an environment of abuse and terror because he can't deal with life and take it out on a woman. Now look, I don't usually get involved with married couple issues, but abuse is a different thing. I'm here if you need me."

I began to cry and when I say cry, I mean really cry uncontrollably. I cried as if I've held a flood of emotions inside of my heart and today my heart said no more and cracked under the pressure of pain. "I can't believe this is happening to me! WHY!!!?"

Tracey just held me. I took advantage of the shoulder. I needed it. Life has taken me through changes since I can remember. I have no clue where my birth mother is, I don't know who my father is. I'm too ashamed to go to my adopted Mom because of fear of the shame I will cause her and the one person I thought I could count on has turned into an enemy. All I have to show for my life now is three kids and high school education. I'm twenty-two years old and lost, all because of a man.

"We have to think of a plan to get you out but, you have to play it cool Leah. No going back. Understood?"

I shook my head in agreement. I was desperate and it didn't matter how I got away from Lewis, I had to get out NOW and Tracey was my Harriet Tubman.

"Ok, good. Now, tell me about this snakes routine."

Chapter 37 [LEAH]

"This is it." I thought after Lewis told me he had to make a run to New Orleans for work. He wouldn't be back for three days and that was more than enough time for me to pack my things and go.

"I'll need some stuff from the store, you think you can do that for me; I have to get back? He asked,

"Yeah, sure." I tried not to have a confused look on my face. My heart was racing at the fact that the door to the prison has flew open. *"Ok, Leah you can't be afraid to fly."* I thought.

Lewis walked out the door and I closed it behind him. He usually would kiss me before he left, but no more. He used to hug me before he left but no more. He would hold me tight and smile and look me deeply in my eyes before he left, but no more. He's already grabbing me, or a quick slap to the face, what's next murder. I began to pray:

Dear God,

"Here I am once again asking for your strength once more

To carry on in your will for what I'm about to do. You see my adversary

and you are my guide.

Forgive me for my sins and purify me

with your blood and come into my life again.

Give me direction. In Jesus name, Amen."

I stood by the window and watched Lewis drive off. As soon as he was out of sight I went into the kitchen. That way, if he makes a U-turn and comes back for "something he forgot" he would think I'm getting something for the kids to eat. I did pack some things for me and the kids to have just in case though but not for the reasons he would think. I placed those items in Juniors backpack. I went and got a duffle bag I had Tracey buy for me and began to pack the kids some items and pack me a few things. You see, I called my mother and told her my troubles. She was so upset to hear of the news:

"Oh honey, what happened?" my mother just groaned. "You gotta get out that situation my dear, we gotta find a way." I can hear the panic in her voice.

"I know Ma, I know. Just calm down, I have a plan. I just need to come home to get myself together." I've haven't been keeping up with checking on Mom as I should. Between trying to fight Lewis the kids and trying to stay on his good side, I got distracted.

"Well c'mon then because this can't be happening to you." She assured me.

I was so scared that my Mom would be disappointed in me. I feel I failed. I had three children and that's it, nothing else to show for the 4 years I've been gone. No other education but a high school diploma, I didn't see how I was going to make it, but I wasn't afraid.

"Here Junior put this on." I handed him a clean shirt for him to put on while I get the twins together. I brought the kids downstairs and had them sit in the living area while I went and called Tracey. "Hey! Yeah, it's me. I'm ready; its time."

"ok, you have any bags or anything?" Tracey asked.

"Yeah, just two so far. The kids are ready." I explained

"ok, I'll walk over and get the bags first just in case he comes rolling back, that way if we have to hustle, they won't slow you down." Tracey explained.

"Alright, see ya when you get here." We hung up from each other. I went to check on the kids and see if they were okay. A few minutes later I heard a knock on the back door. I ran to the back door of the patio and let Tracey in. We got all the bags together and Tracey walked them back to the car.

I watched Tracey go around through the gate out of sight. I went back to the living area where the kids were, and I heard Junior laughing hysterically. When I approached the living area, I could see the twins still in their car seats.

"Wus up Leah?"

"Hey." I was so nervous. "Junior, come to mama."

"SOOO, where you are going?" Lewis started to approach me. I had Junior in front of me trying to figure out a way to get out.

"I was headed to my mother's; you know I haven't seen her in a while and the twins are almost ten months. I just wanted to check on her with her being ill and all." He walked behind me and junior and I turned around facing where the patio's direction was. Thank God we changed positions because Tracey came back into the house and saw Lewis. "I just really miss her Lewis and want to see my mother."

His face softened a little as if he understood. I'm sure he would give up anything to have a chance to see his mother again. Tracey went out the back and kind of signaled me that the car is in the front. "I don't see no harm in that go see your Mom. I'll see you when you get back." He kissed Junior on the forehead and the twins and walked down the hall to our bedroom.

I immediately went and picked up both car seats. I'm not sure where this strength came from, but I was determined not to miss this chance. "C'mon Junior and hurry." I lowered my voice just in case Lewis is around the corner listening. I didn't want him to hear the desperation in my voice. We walked toward the door. I put the twins down and opened the door. I signaled Tracey for help. Before I knew it, we were on our way down the road.

The fresh wind that entered my body was like no other. I felt like I could breathe again, and it felt like being reborn.

Chapter 38 [JAMES]

The first time I saw Denise she was probably in elementary, but I didn't really notice HER until junior prom night. I ended up meeting Marissa there, she didn't want any issues if Leah showed up. She felt the tension at the record store. Denise walked in with this guy I've seen around but didn't know too well. The red in her dress brought out her perfectly almond eyes which were stunning. As I made my way to examine the rest of her aura, Marissa pinched the side of arm.

"Ow, damn girl, that hurt." I rubbed my arm. Marissa pinched like somebody's grandmother. She looked at me and shook her head and continued to drink her punch.

I always thought that she pinched me out of jealousy, but it wasn't. Denise and Leah are best friends I should have not been checking her out in the first place. It's amazing how the understanding of things come to you down the line. I got in line for coffee at a nearby shop and immediately I knew who she was. Still looking stunning as that night at the Jr. Prom. I was scared to say anything so I just played it off and let be what will be.

I felt a sensation go through my body at the sound of the sweetest, sensual voice.

"James?"

My heart was filled with the raindrops of joy. "De-De?"

Chapter 39 [LEAH]

"Don't be weary in prayer; keep at it..." I told myself. I was reading from the book of Colossians to my children. Mom still had my room the same way it was when I left. I always had my bible in my nightstand with pen and pad. It had a lot of highlights and some of the pages were worn but it was still in good condition. Junior finally went to sleep, and the twins were down as well an hour earlier. I took the baby monitor with me and went into the living room where my mother and Tracey were talking over coffee and some crumb cake.

"Hey." I took a long breath before sitting and leaning heavily on the table.

"How you are doing baby?" my mom grabbed my hand. Her hands were cold to the touch which is how I felt the hand I've been dealt in life was: cold but not in a good way.

"I'm better. I'm glad we were able to come. Thanks again Mom, I really appreciate it. Oh, and don't worry he won't come here." I assured her

"I hope not, be as it may with the Lord, but I'll have to shoot 'em." We all laughed.

"I know that's right." Tracey agreed and the laughter subsided and we all just sat at the table in our own thoughts.

Later that night I heard the phone ring and was awaken by the sound. I was already sleeping light anyway because of fear that Lewis would be here dragging me out of my mother's house. I heard mama pick up the phone.

"Hello." She said in a faint voice. She must have fallen asleep in her chair again reading her bible. "whose calling?" "Hmm what do you need son?" At this time, I knew it was Lewis on the other line. "Well she has told me about all the abuse..." "Wait, wait. Let me finish!" she said with a little more volume. "Now, the way you're being disrespectful now goes to show me that you haven't been respecting my daughter's son. Yall have these kids and you supposed to be the example." I just stood there and listened to my mother "preach" to Lewis over the phone. It wouldn't help; he's a stubborn jackass and will stop at nothing to have his way. She finally hung up the phone. I slipped back into my bed because I heard her footsteps. I didn't want her to think I was eavesdropping. "Leah?!" she called out softly. "Leeaahh."

"Yeah, ma?" I replied sitting up in the bed.

"Lewis called and he wants to talk to you. The phone is in the living room I'm going to bed." She added

"Ok, I'll get it." I got out of bed and went into the hall. I walked past the kitchen into the living room. Before I picked up the phone mom was in the kitchen and added.

"Oh, and I talked to him already about his behavior but remember Leah, you don't have to pay the price for someone else when Jesus done did it already." She walked back out the kitchen before also adding. "Remember that!"

"Yes Ma'am," I said softly before picking up the receiver. I took a deep breath and channeled the energy of not giving in. I'm tired of believing the lies, I'm tired of being unappreciated and controlled. I'm tired of being in constant fear of who I am. I want to live my life the way God intended to be. I don't believe this is it and there is something better for me. As I slowly brought the receiver toward my ear, I had a quick thought. *"Why am I taking the time to listen to bondage when I am to be set free from it? Is it because I have confused the feeling of obligation with being under control of my husband?"* All I know what I'm receiving for Lewis now in our marriage is not love and if love is not a midst, I do not want any part of it. I slowly hung up the phone and stepped back. I expected it to ring and for Lewis to be on the other end demanding that I speak to him, but no ring. That was confirmation enough that I am making the right choice; for my children.

I walked back to the room, checked on the kids and kissed each one of them. I slipped back into bed and laid there thinking of where I would go or do now. I have no money, other than the petty cash Lewis gives me on a weekly basis. I had started putting it in another account that he didn't know of for this day. I had to find a skill or trade. With three kids and an abusive husband as their father, it's hard to trust that he would behave their best interest at heart. I'll sleep on it tonight and hopefully it'll be clearer in the morning.

Chapter 40 [DENISE]

Coming back home was bittersweet. I'm not the same person I was when I left. My experiences in life have turned me into another or a new creature. What will create another part of me now? Growing up takes time but the rush to have that feeling of being grown is the desire one must tame.

I had to endure the most painful decision of my life. I asked the Lord to take my life on the way to do it. But what can you do? After ending it with Zedekiah I found out I was pregnant. I thought I coughed up a kidney I was so sick one morning.

[TOILET FLUSHES]

"Uggh!" I walked over to the sink to clean out my mouth and brush my teeth about a thousand times. The scent of the vomit was sickening. It seems like once or twice a week for the past 2 weeks when I eat my taco salad, I get sick. That's unusual I've never gotten sick before. "what's is it?" I groaned out. "this can't be no taco salad." I walked slowly back to the bed and folded myself in the covers. No class for me today.

The next afternoon I took a little walk over to Zedekiah's office. I didn't want to go to his apartment to tell him this. He's been trying to contact me since he decided to end the "arrangement." I didn't want to give him any ideas and here he won't make a scene once he realizes it.

[KNOCK, KNOCK]

Zedekiah looked up from his desk and stood up. He had this confused but kind of remorseful face as if he didn't know whether to be mad at me or forgive me. I'm just guessing, I know he didn't look too pleased. "Denise."

"Zed... I mean Zedekiah." I didn't want to make it personal. "I hope I'm not interrupting..."

"Uh, no. Is there something I can help you with?" he started to take the papers he was reading and placing them in a folder.

"Well..."

"come in, come in." he waved to let me know it was okay.

I walked in as he sat down in his seat. He signaled for me to sit down in the chair across from him. He looked the same, grey eyes, finely trimmed beard; he was a beauty but that's how I got in this situation in the first place. I took a deep breath to calm my nerves and tried to find the words to tell him. "So, are you alright? You look very troubled, Denise." He asked.

"I have something to tell you and I can't seem to bring myself to say it because of fear of your reaction," I explained.

"Just say it, Denise. That's all you can do." He said in a nonchalant manner. Just as I thought not good.

{scoffs} "Ok, I'm pregnant." I sat there looking him straight in the eye. How's that for all I can do.

"What? Pregnant? So, you're saying its mine?" he asked

"So, how's the wife?" I changed the subject to make a point.

Zedekiah leaned back in his chair. "She's good."

"Well, since that is out in the air and we see why you would even ask me that, it's yours. Now I'm coming to you to see what we need to come up with..." I elaborated

"Come up with, you mean money?" he insulted me. I sat there for a minute before responding.

"You know what Zedddd, you need to grow up." I got up out of the chair and started to walk out to leave.

"De-De! Wait!" Zed said

"Nope, nope nope," I said shaking my head, walking out the door. I got in my car and headed back to my apartment that I shared with my roommates.

The next day I woke up, I still felt funny after having the abortion and still bled a little. My soul was messed up but all I could do was continue to pray. Zedekiah made it very clear he didn't want to have anything to do with this pregnancy. He blocked my number after the day I stormed out. That's all it took for me. I thought about my decision. I hardly knew Zedekiah, which is my fault. I'm young and stupid, I guess. People will have their opinions about my decision but since life didn't happen to them in the way life hit me, they feel they can judge. The way the world is going now in 1993 why would I want to raise a child up in this world. Society is fighting against the evils of drugs, police brutality, World Trade Center bombing, the crazy weather that is happening; let alone trying to escape my demons of my parents and hoping to be better than them. All I had was a college education but no means to take care of a child that will grow up once again in a dysfunctional situation and starts its life off with pain and misery from the beginning. Who would want to live in this world? I much rather be with my father in heaven. So, I decided to have one, based on what my twenty-two-year-old mind knew so far to be. I believe God has forgiven me after crying out for days for forgiveness, but I haven't forgiven myself. It is a dark secret that will haunt me for the rest of my life.

All these thoughts race through my head as I was walking in the town center not far from the old neighborhood. It was a sunny, cool day where the leaves show off the magnificent color of green that brightens at the kiss of the sun.

I saw a guy that looked familiar to me. Dark handsome type. I walked up to the counter to make my order for my coffee and sure enough there he was James Detrick. I thought I would never see him again. "James?"

"De-De?" he said with the most excited look on his face.

"Wow, look at you all handsome." I laughed and lightly slapped his shoulder. "I hardly recognized you."

"Yeah, well. How have you been?" he said with a concerned look on his face. It was strange to see him in this element. You can see his growth even though he always had that young boy look, he's a young man now.

"I'm getting by thus far, but nothing God can't handle. How about you, on your way to your own practice are we?" I asked as we began to walk slowly down the "Courtyard Town Centers" sidewalks of shops and eateries.

"A while for that, I'm doing an internship through NYU." He smiled a nervous smile.

"Well that's great, I mean why the uncertainty?"

"What do you mean?" he stopped and looked at me.

"Well by your response, you seem to have a little anxiety or doubt of some kind," I added. I hope I didn't offend James. This was one of the most interesting conversations I had with a guy in a long time. I guess that's why I was attracted to the professor because of his intellect. You live and you learn; what you like.

"Hm, maybe. I have set a high expectation for myself; I believe. And now I'm afraid it's going to blow up in my face because of all the past transgressions of mine. Stupid huh?"

I started to reminisce about the conversations I used to have with Nathan. The last voicemail I received from him I ignored:

Hey,
I need you to call me at home now.
It's been 24 hours and I can't make it without you.
I apologize for making you feel not needed
and underappreciated. I pray you forgive me.
I love you and again, I'm sorry. {BEEP}

"No, not at all," I replied. Who am I to talk about anybody's transgressions right now? We stopped and caught a glance of each other for a moment.

[scoffs] "It was nice seeing you, Denise. Thanks for listening." He said as he tapped my forearm with the hand, he was holding his coffee.

"Oh, no problem. Nice seeing you as well. Well, I better get going to wherever it was I was going." I said with an awkward laugh to match. I wasn't sure what was going on here, but I wanted out of the whole scene.

"Oh okay, no problem. Uh, maybe I'll see ya before you head back." He inquired

"Maybe." I smiled and waved. "See ya later James." I turned and walked away. I had too much to deal with currently in my life. I needed direction. It would feel good to have someone near that can hold e at this time. To rub my head and let me know that everything will be okay. But this is a road I must take by myself. Running to the comfort of another to cover another problem can no longer be a pattern for me to follow.

I walked around the town center a bit longer trying to figure out which path in life I should have not turned down and what path should I take now. I believe if I keep thinking about the positive things in life the love and affection that I have for myself deep within can and will heal me. If it's not one thing I do have and that's perseverance.

"The race is not given to the swift nor given to the strong."
I thought. I decided to call it a night and see what the
morning brings.

Chapter 41 [LEWIS]

I got permission from Leah's mom to come by so I can talk to her. Yeah, I've been the biggest asshole and I want to make it right. I just don't know how. I love Leah so much, but I believe my love for her is what is damaging this relationship. I have issues of control and anger lately. I've never seen my Dad raise his hand to my mother, I'm just in a place of failure and I can't cope. I got in my truck and headed over to see Leah and my children. She has been silent, and it is becoming unbearable. No phone call to let me know if she is okay or if my kids are okay. She's gone too far.

I walked up to the porch and rang the doorbell. Ms. Moses' feet swept across the floor slowly, letting me know she was not in any rush to let me in. She opened the door after opening the curtain to inspect her porch. I saw her look me up and down through the screen.

"Hey son, wait right there. I'll go get Leah."

"Damn." I thought. I can't come in the house at least. I guess I would be furious too. But what happened to second chances.

I saw Leah walking toward the door and my heart started to race in excitement and fear of the rejection I know was coming. She did not have a welcoming look on her face once she lifted her eyes to see me. There was no glimpse of sunshine, the same sunshine I was used to seeing every day in the beginning. I had literally crushed her, and it took me being away from her to realize what I had.

"We need to talk," I said. I should have asked but it just came out like that.

"About?" she said coldly

This pissed me off a little, so I decided just to say how I felt. "About you leaving this weekend. Because you just can't get mad Leah and decide to leave and not communicate with me. It's just not acceptable. I'm still your husband. Now, if you need some time then just say that. I've given you free passes on a lot of stuff because I know I'm hard to live with right now. With the kids and new area, there were some adjustments for all of us. I know I've mistreated you and I'm sorry. Now, if this is too much for you and you want to leave then we need to discuss things like adults. I understand I hurt you, but this is not the way."

She stood there looking at me with no expression. I didn't know what to think. "anything else?"

"Yeah. I love you and miss you and I apologize for not listening to you and supporting you more with the kids. And I am especially sorry forever raising a hand to you. I am truly, truly sorry. Please forgive me" I begged of her. She had no expression on her face. Then for a moment she lifted her head and looked me straight into my eyes:

"Everything that I do to stand beside you is more than you can ever imagine. And since I am human some things are going to get neglected. I was just tired of it being me. So, I chose me. I was torn between choosing one or the other: all the things that you love that I do for you in its entirety and neglect myself or love me so that you can be who you are without me being you." Then she said the most hurtful but truthful thing:

"You can beat yourself up for your mom leaving you so early in your life but not me. Not anymore. Just because she's gone doesn't mean she's far away. I'm sure she watches over you Lewis. But, do you think she would approve, do you, do you think this is the son she wanted?"

I couldn't do anything but put my hands in my pocket and hold my head down in shame.

"DO YOU?" she yelled before the tears started to roll down her face. She has never raised her voice at me before in such anger. I had no idea how I was going to come back from this. I think I've gone too far. The one who was made to be with me to help me is saying she no longer can, so now I must help myself.

Leah sniffled a little, "Just as I thought, I have nothing more to say. Do as you wish." She had an aloof look for a moment before wiping her eyes. "Goodbye." She backed up from the porch back into the house and closed the door.

I've never felt so alone.

Chapter 42 [NATE]

When I met the love of my life, I tried to imagine it as a bright sunny day, the typical cliché but knowing me and every path I've taken it would just end up with me seeing her and in some adversity. While talking to Marissa, we took a break to see if this is what we both wanted. It was about six months before we spoke again. During that time, I did a lot of things to try to get over Denise and to also see if Marissa would move on. I started running every morning and eating better, making dishes that I liked to do that were healthier. I started to look for spaces with help from my Dad. So, one day while at home in my apartment I decided to call Denise. It was like digging up a dead body, scary as hell. But, I did it.

[RING]

"Hello." I smirked [scoffs a little] "you know how?" I replied

Of course, she asked me what I needed or how I got her number. She should know me better than that. It sounded like she was sleeping. We talked some more about what's been going on in her life. I can hear the clank of a spoon hitting a coffee cup in the background. Same old Denise boogie as hell, but I love her. Come to find out she's been talking to James, that's all I need in my life. I'm not sure if I should let Marissa know that. I'm not sure if they were really friends or what. I'll think about it later.

Well, Denise and I have gone on enough for me to seek the closure I needed. "Denise?"

"Yes," she answered.

"I called to let you know…"

Chapter 43 [MARISSA]

I told Nate about my encounter with James. I can tell he felt some type of way which we're on this "break" is why things got a little heated but not bad, so we just needed some time. I'm still carrying on with my plans, I'm ready to get out of Waller County anyway. I've been holding off with sleeping with Nate. I'm trying to get my life back on track. I took it really slow with Nate. I mean really slow after that day in the car. He was patient, which led me to believe he must care at least. Who doesn't need a friend?

"Do you usually talk to him or is this a first encounter?" he asked.

"No, Nate. I see him but I do avoid him. This is the first time he's been successful at catching me off guard." I didn't know what was in his mind. He looks like he thought I was joking with him or something. "Nate, he said what he said, I accepted the apology. It's closed. What's the issue babe?

He walked toward me with a look doubt. "Well, we are about to do something that would bring us closer or farther apart. Do we have any past issues that haven't been closed with past loves?" he asked.

"I never looked at it like that. Well, I closed mine today. Do you? What about Denise?" I asked. I knew Denise from elementary school and she and Leah were best friends, but I never dealt with Denise to build a friendship.

"No, I haven't talked to her in a while. There's no need to." I replied wondering where this was headed.

"Well, for you to feel some type of way about me just telling you about James. Do you trust me that I wouldn't do that to you?" I asked. I never had a second thought on where Nate was or is he telling me the truth about who he was with. We were in a distant relationship. I had to wrap my mind around the fact that things change. People change. Growth can be a bitch.

"I do, I just still have doubts sometimes of course, not about you in particular." He looked up as he was just seeing the light. "I just have doubts about our lives coming together and what if our journeys turn for the worst and that's not being together." He came closer and held both my hands.

"Well, maybe you should take some time and decide. I'll be here." I proclaimed. Maybe this time will give me the time I need to adjust to Houston and see if Nate and I should continue, or at least give us a fresh start.

"I really don't want that, Marissa."

"No, all we're doing is taking some time to make sure this is the right thing for both of us to further our relationship. To make sure if we both want the same things." I explained with much sincerity. I hoped he understood. We stood by his car a little longer hugging each other. I also hoped he will come back to me.

Chapter 44 [LEAH]

My relationship with Denise is kind of a long distant one. We went from being best friends to long distant friends. The love is still there but the presence in our relationship is missing. So much has happened in our lives that it hindered the both of us from each other.

I finally got Denise's number from her mom. She was still in Washington D.C. starting her internship.

"Hello." She answered. She seemed to be more upbeat than usual.

"Hey, De-De its Leah."

"OH, hey girl. How have you been?" she seemed shockingly surprised.

"Oh, a lot. You seemed surprised and happy?" I noticed.

"Well, yeah it's been a long time. You and Lewis living the life in that big house of yours I hardly get to see you or hear from you. But I'm glad I can hear from you now. So, tell me. What's up?" There was an awkward silence on the phone before Denise broke it. "Leah, you okay?"

I wanted to tell her of all the trials that love has sent me thru. Losing love has shown me what love truly is. Denise's tone was not that of someone I wanted to trust my most intimate secrets with. Maybe we have grown apart.

"Have you heard from James?" I asked to change the subject.

"Oh!" she said with a slight pause. "Hold on a minute." I couldn't hear too much background noise just a male's voice slowly approaching the other end of the receiver.

"Hey." Said, James.

I fell back into my chair not knowing what to think. James's voice was ringing in my ear so, that I began to have a headache. Here ittttts my so-called best friend and my first love. So many questions started to form in my head.

[CLICK]

I hung up the phone without saying a word.

Chapter 45 [LEAH]

Who am I? I'm whoever you want me to be or can be who I want to be. To be in love with someone even after the hurt can be a confusing time. The only thing on my mind was to rid myself of Lewis, rid myself of my friends' disappointment, rid myself of my hatred, anger, and love for my biological mother. I wanted to cleanse myself of the self-hate, doubt, fear, hurt and loneliness that I feel right now. I have my children but only part of the day. I'm still with my mother, Ms. Moses but I found a part-time job at a beauty salon that my mother goes to. I shampoo on occasion and mainly keep the place tidy. I'm grateful for this job for now having three kids' money can be scarce overnight. I still have some of the money I had withdrawn before leaving Lewis.

I started going to cosmetology school three days a week. My mom is retired so she helps watch the kids while I'm at school. The best thing about working in the salon the daycare center is there so the kids can come with me to work. I was pretty good at this trade so I figured why not and even if it didn't work out, I can branch off from it somehow. This can do until I get my child support together with Lewis.

I befriended one of the young ladies that worked in the shop. She's been there a while, I'm not sure if she is related to the owner or not but she sure gets away with a lot. She was the main shampoo girl, still in college; just here to get a little change while in school. She said she loved the hours. I would usually see her on Saturdays which is the earliest and only shift 7:30a – 2p. She was pretty good. Her scissor game was on point. I walked in at about 7:45a, one of the twins got up early. This Saturday I was off but wanted to get a new cut. I just used the same time I would get up, that way the ids would stay on schedule.

"Good morning girl," I said with a sigh of relief that I made it safe. The bus is crazy.

"Hey, Le-Le. You alright?" she said with a little laugh.

"Yeah, just got off that crazy bus. I got the hair for my braids, where you want it?"

"Just. Sit it over there." She pointed toward another station next to hers. This was going to be a slow day for her, so she squeezed me in. "So, how are you adjusting, school ok?"

Everything appeared to be aligning well. I had help from mom and the fact that I can be close to help if she needed anything is better. Lewis Jr started kindergarten this year and is adjusting well. The twins are developing on schedule. There is not much to complain about. I finally feel free. "Yeah, everything is fine. Just fine."

Chapter 46 [JAMES]

A true friend is life's little blessing. Friendship can develop with a person you would have never thought. Denise and I have been communicating on a regular basis. She's been a blessing in disguise. She started her internship at Psych Institute in Washington, and she's been nervous about it. Who could blame her? This NYU internship is not a walk in the park either. I believe I'm leaning toward family therapy.

It was the 4th of July weekend and I took a trip to D.C. to hand out with her for the weekend. I mean she lives in the nation's capital. Why not? Denise and I hung out and had a great time. There was music, food, live performances; it was an awesome day. Denise looked exceptional! We haven't taken any steps toward being more than friends or do I know if I will. All I know is that I enjoy her company and conversation. Our personalities just match as friends.

"Having a good time?" Denise yelled over the loud music to be heard. She was dancing to the music in place. She had a good groove going on. The DJ was playing Erykah Badu's "On & On.

"Oh, Yeah! I'm loving it. Thanks for inviting me." I said in her ear.

"Sure, you think I was going to let you stay in New York all by yourself this weekend." She grabbed my arm and hugged it. I just laughed along. It did feel good to have someone to really care about you enough to take the time to check up on you. I guess that's what I liked about Denise she not only knew how to articulate her feelings she knew how to show them. Genuine. "Please, then I needed the company too."

"Oh, so I'm being used De-De?" I teased.

"No! I wouldn't do that James." She gave me a sly look and rolled her eyes a little. "There are some people in this world that genuinely just want to show love to people. I'm one of them, no strings attached. That's my friendship to you, James."

Wow! Denise's whole essence changed. I never took the time to get to know someone. It made me think of what I wanted in my life right now instead of just letting life spiral in a whirlwind. We walked a few more blocks to the apartment that Denise and her roommate shared. She wanted to show off some of her paintings and books she's been writing on top of studying at her internship. I had a good time hanging out with Denise. [RING, RING] She went to go answer her phone.

"Hold on James." She reached over the couch for the phone. I nodded as to understand. The conversation was short.

"Hello." She answered.

"OH, hey girl. How have you been?" she looked at me with a shockingly surprised look on her face. I had mouth to her:

"What?"

"Well, yeah it's been a long time. You and Lewis living the life in that big house of yours I hardly get to see you or hear from you." Denise adjusted herself on the couch. "But I'm glad I can hear from you now. So, tell me. What's up?" There was an awkward silence and Denise's face looked as if she was waiting on something to come out of thin air. "Leah, you okay?" she asked.

My heart dropped a little and I almost spit out the apple juice Denise gave me when we came in. I put my drink down on the coffee table and brushed off my shirt to see if I spilled some of the juice.

"Oh!" Denise said then she mouthed to me:

"She just asked about you?"

"Hold on a minute." Denise put her hand over the receiver and handed to me. I pushed it away waving my hands mouthing:

"No, no man. I ain't ready"

"James! Take this phone and see what's up? She may need you. "she said quietly. Denise got up off the couch and walked in the kitchen and signaled me to follow her so I can talk to Leah.

I took a deep breath and got off the couch and walked over to Denise and took the phone from her. "Okay, okay," I told Denise. I put the receiver to my ear and took a deep breath. "Hey."

There was silence and then a dial tone. I stood there in disbelief for a while. "Denise!"

"Yeah!"

"She hung up." I looked at the receiver as if it was its fault. Denise walked back into the kitchen with a confused look on her face.

"She asked about you so I don't understand why she would do that."

"She ASKED about me?" I said in disbelief.

"Yeah. She asked, 'have I heard from you' and I thought maybe you would like to hear from her. Did I do something wrong?" Denise was right.

Chapter 47 [JAMES]

I wanted to talk to Leah, I just didn't know where to begin. I still missed her kind voice even after all this time. I've been concerned about her being with Lewis, I know what kind of temper he has. After his Mom passed, he was just a walking time bomb of anger. It was devastating to hear of their marriage, but I still wished her the best and I will always be here for her.

I arrived back in New York, a little tired from the weekend festivities but not exhausted. Denise gave me the number that came up on her caller ID from when Leah called. I'm sitting here in my apartment looking at this number trying to decide if I should call Leah or not. The way she hung up I can't tell if it was something wrong or she was not ready as well. I had so many questions, but I wasn't sure if I'm ready for the answers.

Chapter 48 [DENISE]

"What are you talking about Leah?"

"You know damn well what I'm talking about!"

Leah and her stories, I think she really believes love is like those poems she writes. All fairytales.

"No, I don't. I called you back to see why you hung up on James and to make sure everything was okay. It was strange of you to do that." I explained.

"How would you know what's strange of me to do anything. I haven't seen or heard from you in I don't know how long. You were supposed to be my friend." She cried out.

"AND SO WERE YOU!" I couldn't help myself. I needed Leah at moments over the past few years and she was nowhere to be found.

There was silence and the sound of sniffles in the background from Leah. Even though it's been a while since we've talked, I still know when there is something wrong.

"Then why James, huh why him?" she sounded so hurt but I was still confused.

"What? What do you mean 'why James'?"

"You and him being together Denise. Don't play crazy." She said a little firmly.

I thought about what she said and the whole incident of him being at my place and then the light bulb went off. She was under the impression that James and I were together. My poor friend always jumping to conclusions.

"Oh my God, Nooo Le-Le! James and I are not together. We're friends just like we've always been. Is that what you thought…. oh, my goodness." I laughed and put my hand on my head.

"Oh! I guess I did jump a little." She said quietly.

"You mean LEAPED." I chuckled. Then she chuckled. "I've missed you, friend." We said in unison.

Chapter 49 [TRACEY]

With each waking moment, I crave his love, I crave being in his whole being. The way he massages me from head to toe until all the love I have burst out in moans of ecstasy. I can't get enough and finally you're all mine. To have and to hold but then why must you run from it. Why must you keep secrets? My heart aches at your continuous slopes and dips while you go down on me knowing this will be something, I must keep to myself.

"AHHHH! WHAT THE FUCK?"

"LEAH?!!!!!!!"

Chapter 50 [JAMES]

I finally got the nerve to call Leah. I just had to face the truth. Throughout the years there is not a day that went by that I didn't think of her at least once. She will always be my girl.

"Hey, James. How are you?" She sounded so sweet. When she picked up, I didn't say anything for a while. I guess she read the caller ID.

"Hey, don't hang up. Please." I said jokingly but seriously.

"I won't." She chuckled a little. "Sorry about that, De-De explained everything."

"Well, me and Denise are not..."

"I know." She interrupted.

"And we were jus…."

"James, it's okay." She laughed.

It was so much I wanted to say. "Remember this."

"What is it that you do

Wanting to be where you are

And you haven't got a clue

I'm in love with you

Your light just seems so far

There so many things to tell you

> *So, I'll just wish upon a star*
>
> *Hope it aligns me back to you*
>
> *Because I'm in love with you."*

[Leah sniffles]

"Yeah, I remember. Ugh, stupid right?" I hated when she didn't see the beauty within her.

"No, not at all." I absorbed the moment of having my friend back. I missed her so. "What's going on with you? Is everything ok?"

"I'm not gonna lie to you. No. No its not." She said

She went on to explain all the turmoil she's been thru with Lewis. She kept things a secret for face value, but it backfired. She did feel she was forced to be with him because of the kids but she couldn't take any more of the abuse. This made me furious. I knew it. "Bastard." Is the only thing I could say regarding her situation.

"Don't be mad James, I knew I should have gotten out way before now and tried to hold on hoping he would change. But, I'm in a better place now. I just have one problem." She added.

"What Leah, just ask?" I wanted to help in any way I could and if I could get a chance to get my hand on Lewis punk ass, all the better.

"I'm moving to my new place finally."

"Oh, wonderful Leah." I tried to make her feel encouraged.

"Thank you, but there are some things that were left at the house I wanted for the kids and I need Lewis's social security number. He won't answer my calls since I won't come back. I plan on filing for divorce as soon as I can have an adequate living arrangement and a steady job for face value." She explained.

I knew what she meant. She was still his wife and she wanted to make sure her kids lived in a place that was decent. Obviously, he's not helping so she wants to see what she can get. "well how do you propose we do this Leah?" I was down. I know Leah did everything for that negro.

"I still have a copy of the keys. I made them just in case. Now, I'm not sure if he changed the locks but knowing his arrogance, he still thinks I'll be back, begging." She said

"Well, I'll be home next month to visit my parents. We can meet up then?" I proposed

"Are you serious James?" she asked in disbelief.

"I'll call and let you know when to expect me. See ya then. Love you, Leah."

Chapter 51 [LEWIS]

Each day my secret eats at me tearing me apart from the inside out. Leah was my everything to endure it. She was the one that made it easier each day to get by. Once again, the monster in my closet showed its ugly head.

Tracey had been living next door to us for about a year before we ever spoke. Uneasy I felt when Tracey was around, I was still cordial and kept the peace. Leah seemed to get too familiar with the two of them in the garden all the time.

"Hey, Lewis."

"Tracey." I nodded as a gesture to keep it moving. I stood at the end of the back porch sipping the sweet tea that Leah made earlier.

"Hot day isn't it?" Tracey began chit-chatting.

I stood and turned to go up the stairs to the house. "Yep!"

Tracey grabbed my arm. "Real hot."

"Hey, you two!" Leah walked toward the porch area. I quickly let go of Tracey's hand on my arm. "What's wrong with yall?" Leah looked back and forth at the two of us for an answer.

"Oh, nothing girl. I was just telling Lewis about, how he can be out here with all those work clothes on and it is so hot." Tracey lied.

"I'm just aggravated, that's all." I walked back in the house and put my glass on the table. I went into the hallway bathroom and closed the door. "Get it together Lewis," I said in the mirror. I washed and dried my face and took some long deep breaths.

Here I am again being seduced in my own home where my children and wife used to sleep. I should feel ashamed but then I can't control the feeling. It had been a long day and on time Tracey was waiting on me in the kitchen with a meal. Our daily lunch meetups have become a regular thing now. Not just for sex but for other things as well.

"You want me to stop? You seem tense." Tracey asked

"No, No. I'm good. A lot on my mind ya know." I replied barely. Tracey was giving me head like no other. I couldn't get Leah to go down on me for nothing. I never thought I would get it this way though.

I was on my way to ecstasy when I heard ringing in my ear.

"AHHHH! WHAT THE FUCK?"

I looked around and I saw Leah and James standing across in the family room facing the kitchen.

"LEAH?!!!!!!!"

I hurried and pulled up my pants and Tracey ran off to the other side of the kitchen.

James' eyes were wider than the ocean. He quickly exited the kitchen area. "Um, I'll let you talk Leah. I'll be right in this hallway."

Leah was standing there with her fist balled up and eyes red with fury. I continued to put on the rest of my clothes. "Leah. Let me explain, ok"

"Explain what Lewis, huh, WHAT?" she yelled

"I know this is confusing." I tried to explain but Leah was not having it.

"Confusing? Confusing? Calculus is confusing, maybe trying to read a map but I know what I saw!" she walked a little closer. Her face showing me that she was not for it today.

"What do you want me to say, Leah?"

"Oh, I don't know Lewis how about... [mimics a conversation]

> *You: Hi my name is Lewis*
>
> *Me: HI Lewis*
>
> *You: Oh, just to let you know, IM GAY!*

How about that Lewis, how about that?" she said

"I'm not gay, Leah." I tried to explain. "it's jus..."

"I JUST CAUGHT MY HUSBAND GETTING HIS DICK SUCKED BY ANOTHER MAN!!! STOP PLAYIN WITH ME LEWIS!" she was furious. "you know what?" she put up both hands and stepped back. James walked back into the kitchen.

"You alright?" he asked Leah. I noticed his hand placed on the mid of her back.

"Yeah. You know what, just get me out of here." She said to James.

"Leah, I'm sorry!" I pleaded with her. She just put her hand up in my direction and walked away with James.

Chapter 52

[LEAH & JAMES]

We walked back to the car and got in. To say the least, we were both shocked. Sitting there with a million thoughts cycling through our heads, you can feel the tension, despair, hurt and anger in the air.

"Let's just get out of here, maybe get a drink," I suggested. Leah just put her face in her hands and started to cry. I couldn't imagine the pain she must be going thru. I've known Lewis for quite some time but not in a million years did I think he was on the under. I was speechless.

I rubbed her back softly, "How could I not see? I'm just the dumbest person alive. Why do bad things keep happening to me?"

"Leah. This is not your fault. C'mon let's just go." I put the keys in the ignition and started the car. I took one last look at Leah before I backed up from the driveway. She looked tired and just fed up and just about ready to give up.

"I don't care where we go just get me far away from this dreadful place." She leaned her seat back and covered her forehead with her hand. "I have a splitting headache."

We found a bar not too far up the street. It was small and intimate which was just enough for us to sit and just process what we just witnessed. We walked in and found a table in a corner. Leah was afraid of being seen with bloodshot swollen eyes from all the crying she had been doing in the car. As we sat down a waiter came over.

"Water please and a cape cod." I nudged Leah to get her attention. "What do you want Leah?"

"The same, it doesn't matter," Leah responded. She didn't even lookup.

"Two of the same please," I told the waiter.

"Ok, I'll bring those right out." Said the waiter as she walked away. She tried to not notice Leah's behavior, but it was obvious.

"Leah, baby. C'mon." I pulled her closer so she could lean on my shoulder. I put my chin on her head. "Why didn't you call me, or tell me what you were going thru, you know I would have been there for you? No matter what."

"What was I supposed to say? I didn't know if you still cared or what, I was scared."

This is true so much has happened, and people do change. But the one thing that has never change is how I feel about Leah. I feel we were destined to be. "I understand."

The waiter came with our drinks. "Thank you," Leah told the waiter. She began to down her water as if its been weeks since she had any.

I laughed a little. "Thirsty?" I just smiled at her. It was nice to see her again.

"A little." She chuckled. "I don't get too much time to myself, so I rush everything. Between school, working and three kids, I'm a little out of touch." She put her head down as if she was ashamed.

"No, no, I didn't mean it like that." I touched her chin and lifted her head. I sipped my drink and just looked at her.

"Thanks for coming James, this means a lot to me." She picked up her cape cod and sipped it. "I didn't get anything from the house, but I guess I would have needed the support. Jesus!" she gave me that old Leah look when we would be thinking the same thing back in school. It was refreshing to see.

"Right?!?!" I said while looking around as if we just saw area 51. "Eww!" I was trying to get the image out of my head. "I might need another drink before its over with. Damn!" I shook my body as if I was trying to get something off me.

"Wait until I tell Denise. She is going to be livid." She said. "Oh my God, my kids James. My kids, what am I supposed to tell them?"

I leaned back in the booth and folded my arms. I had no answer for her on that one. That would be the most difficult thing for me to do if I were in her situation. "I don't know Leah." I shook my head a little trying to think of something. Leah leaned back in the booth as well still holding her drink she signaled to the waiter.

"Can we have two more of these please?"

"Sure." The waiter looked surprised by Leah's more upbeat demeanor.

"Oh, and water. More water." She looked as if she was in a trance. "Thanks"

"Leah, I'm here for whatever you need." I took hold of her hand. "Ok?" She looked at me with her big brown eyes. I can see that she already knew she could count on me. I can see the adversity in her face, her expressions. The uncertainty of love and all it has to offer; she has been thru it. I just hope she gives me the chance to restore her faith in love.

Chapter 53 [LEAH]

The days seemed brighter and burdens grew lighter, like the feeling after a battle is won. I mattered to somebody or there is someone in the clouds that intended these things to happen for me to go higher.

After about a year of fighting with Lewis in court, I finally received my divorce papers officially declaring me a single woman. Free from the rule of my dictator husband, free to find me again, free to care for my children the way I see fit. I'm free to, dare I say it; love again.

James and I have been communicating more than ever. He's still in New York but will be coming back home to work. He got offered a position within a psychiatric practice for family counseling and then his plan is to eventually open his own practice, but he felt to start out this way before he just took a leap.

Meanwhile, Lewis gets more demanding by the day. He made it in the divorce where I cannot take the kids across state lines unless we both approve of the matter. Of course, he makes it difficult for me. He knows Lewis and I have reunited so each time I tried to discuss with him of going out of state whether it's with the kids or just me he creates a whole argument of how I'm taking his children away or he thinks they won't be safe. How dare he? Safe? It's hard enough that I must grant him visitation even with his violent past and lifestyle but to suggest that my kids would not be safe with ME after all he's done is ridiculous. He's such a hypocrite.

"You're being unreasonable Lewis."

"How, huh? If I don't feel comfortable with the situation, why must I agree?" he stressed.

"It's not about you feeling comfortable, just admit it. You don't want me to be happy and definitely with James."

"I don't give a rat's ass about no damn James. As far as I'm concerned yall deserve each other but my kids won't be involved."

I chuckled a little at the fact he tried to hide the fact that he's upset about it. "So, I guess it's okay for my kids to be around the environment you've created? Lewis please!"

"Take my kids out of state if you want to. It'll be the last time you see them." He threatened.

"You're pathetic. Bad enough you've sent this family thru all types of hell, fear and might I add DECEPTION; now you don't want us to live our lives? The hell with you Lewis and everything you stand for. You will not try to take control of me nor our kids just because you're confused about who you are and seem to not have any control over that." I hung up the phone. I was tired of trying to be reasonable with him.

James had bought the kids and I tickets to come to New York for Labor Day weekend. I thought it was a nice gesture and the kids and I would love to get out of Louisiana for a change. I asked my mother about it, but she suggested to keep the kids to make sure Lewis won't act a fool about them being gone. He will find anything to still fuss about me being out of town without the kids, but he doesn't need to know everything. He's not my damn daddy.

Chapter 54 [DENISE]

"You got to be kidding me?" I said in shock. I couldn't believe what I was hearing. I must say, back home has changed a whole lot. I can't believe what Leah was telling me about Lewis and her neighbor. And in front of James. I didn't mean to, but I laughed from a healthy place. What are the odds? "Lewis, womanizing Lewis?" I laughed again. "So far, I've seen it all." I leaned back into the chair of my lover.

"He used to make love to me like he wanted to devour me, I had no idea De-De. I HAD NO IDEA!!! [sighs in frustration] "This Mutha--." [deep breath] "I've been through hell and back with this man, and now this!?" she cried out.

This phone conversation was about to get mystical, bottom of the ocean, deep. Let the waters flow. "Leah, don't cry." I paused a little to let her get it out. It takes some time for Leah to let loose and get it off her chest but sooner or later it comes out. And this was the straw that broke the camel's back as we country folks would say. "Are the kids there with you?"

"No, why?" she sniffled.

"Good, take this time to search for Leah. It's not the longest period but try being a little selfish this weekend. Live a little Le-Le! Like you said you've been through hell and back. Just take some time to do whatever it is you want to do. If it's sleeping all day; do that. If it's…" I almost did a slight slip of the tongue but caught myself. "anything, you've earned it dear."

I tried to encourage Leah as much as I could. She was a beautiful person inside and out and it's a shame someone tried to destroy that which God created. I hope she can move on from this experience and find peace.

Chapter 55 [TRACEY]

I haven't been able to see Lewis since the discovery of his hidden secret by Leah and her friend. He's been avoiding my calls or when I see him outside, he rushes off. He's even put the house up for sale. I'm not in love with Lewis by any means. And the help I gave Leah benefitted her. I could tell that fool was on the low the first day we met. He couldn't look me in the eye.

"You okay Lewis?" Leah asked as she struggled with their eldest son.

"Yeah, Yeah. Sorry, but we have to go." He scooped up those twins and hurried toward the house.

"Oh, no problem I understand. You got your hands full there." I brushed it off.

"It was nice meeting you, Tracey." Leah shook my hand. At least somebody had some home training. I knew from the beginning she could do better. "Maybe I'll take you up on that offer for gardening tips after all."

Lewis and I just sort of happened. One thing led to another and bam we're all over each other. All I want to do is just let him know that no harm is done and to clear the air. But it seems no use in doing that. He takes the childish approach and avoids the issue. He'd much rather live the lie than be free.

I did feel bad about hurting Leah in this way but also, I'm glad she knows the truth and like I've always thought. She could do better. Always!

Chapter 56 [LEWIS]

Selling the house was bittersweet for me for one its where I tried to have a family and failed and the reason why I failed was living next door. Tracey was annoying the hell out of me. I know he wanted to talk but I'm done. There's nothing to say. I know he had a hand in helping Leah leave because he's a conniving, backstabbing FA-.

All I'm saying is that I'm not gay and that's what I am sticking with. If my father would find out, I think he would just crumble. What my dad doesn't know is that Mom already knew. That's the only thing that she kept from my Dad. She asked me to reveal myself when I was ready not because I felt forced to. Whomever I sleep with is my business, I don't need to broadcast it everywhere. God already knows.

The possibility of not seeing my kids must be my punishment. I have not been able to get in contact with Leah to talk to her or at least talk to my children; I'm still their father. I already know she's dealing with James. He's the reason for this whole thing in the first place. Since the beginning of time James has been a barrier between Leah and me. I know she still cared for him in some way. If he's around my children, let's just say the situation can turn bloody if need be.

I had moved into an apartment shortly after. I decided to rent in the city downtown area to be close to the main building for the business. I had majority of the stuff from the house to furnish my apartment. The other stuff I put in storage. Leah didn't want anything from me but child support not even my last name. That was quite hurtful but if that's what she wanted who am I to deny her that after what I put her thru.

I tried calling Leah again. I paced as I was anticipating another repeat of her voicemail that I have been listening to for the past couple of weeks. The line clicked and I can hear someone on the other end breathing hard into the phone. I immediately got teary-eyed because I knew it was one of the twins.

"Hey, hey can you hear me?" I asked the child hoping for some type of response.

I can hear Leah in the background. "Leanna! No honey, give me that."

"Hello?" Leah said. I swallowed hard. All the hurt and pain I caused her came rushing back thru me at the sound of her voice.

"Uh, Hey, it's me, Lewis," I said with the uncertainty of if she would hang up or not.

"Mm-hm, what?" it sounded like she was eating something. I decided to call her a little earlier than usual maybe she'll be in a better mood. Leah used to sing in the mornings while making breakfast so I figured the Lord may soften her heart a little to at least hear me out.

"Leah, just listen to me for one minute. I'm sorry, do YOU have a minute to listen?" I corrected myself.

"Go 'head." She said coldly.

"The very first time I saw you I knew you were the one for me. I just got caught up in my own sins and those of my fathers toward my mother. You see growing up, my father would abuse my mother. Not all the time but enough."

"Once is enough Lewis."

"You're right, you're right. I'm still learning to rearrange that Leah. Bear with me please?" I asked

"Fine." She sighed.

"You reminded me so much of her; her patience and kindness. I miss the gentle yet strong way of letting me know when I'm not living right. But most of all her humbleness made me feel I wasn't alone in this world. She made me feel just as important to the best things in life like the next man. And to me Leah, you're the best thing that life can ever give a man. I love you. I know this other side of me is a violation of what we had promised to each other and I apologize for that. I should have let you know my weaknesses and…"

"Its fine, Lewis. Don't go any further. All I can say is I hope you take this time to really look deep inside yourself and see what the learning experience was from this period in your life." She bluntly said. She seemed to not really be interested in what I had to say but then listened out of respect that we have children. "I presumed you were also calling concerning the children?"

"Yes, I was." She let me speak to Junior. He did say too much since it's been a while since I've seen them. The twins played around on the phone with the cord. It was so nice to hear their voices. "Leah, is there any way we can put our differences aside and arrange some type of visitation for my kids? I miss them so much and despite the type of husband I was you know I was a damn good father."

She took a deep breath. "Look, I have been thinking and I definitely do not want my children to grow up not knowing their father or any relatives for that matter. I know how that is to feel like you don't quite belong." She took another deep breath. This was not like Leah to just come out and say exactly what she feels. "And to add to you being a good father; Well…you were alright." she scoffed. Her making a little joke meant her heart had softened but I'm not sure how much.

"So, does that mean I can come get them this weekend? I tested the waters.

"How about for starters, we meet up with the kids for a few hours at Chuckie Cheese or something like that." She suggested. I didn't like the suggestion. I guess my visits with my children, my seeds are supervised now.

"For starters? Does that mean I will not always be supervised? I couldn't help the pettiness.

She laughed a little. "I haven't seen you in months, I'm not sure what you've been up to or what type of life you chose. Just like you had "concerns" about me taking the kids out of state, I have concerns about leaving them with you. I think that is only fair, don't you?"

I'm not sure who this new Leah was. I remember a time where it was easier to get her to back down. Leah was a bit of a people pleaser and I admit I did take advantage of that at times. "Yeah, it's fair. I paused a little to process the reality of Leah not being in my life as my wife. The reality of my transformation into a better man had officially started. My behavior was unwarranted

I'll call you back about the time I can come and see if that's alright with you, Cool?"

"Sure. Goodbye." The click of her hanging up felt like the loneliness of being in a dark cave waiting on someone or something to appear.

I know this feeling will pass with each passing day, the feeling of having everything snatched from under you, the compass you had in your head re-calibrated and you realize you were on the wrong path. Growing up comes at its own pace because everyone is running a different race.

I will now live my life the best way I know how. Because it is the best thing that I can do.

Chapter 57 [LEAH]

The story of boy found girl, boy loses girl, now goes through hell to get her back is where James and I are now. But how far do you let a person continue to prove themselves repeatedly that they love you and they are sorry? My trip to New York was wonderful and I had a great time, I just don't want to move too fast. I had to let James know this before he moved back home to start his new career. Truthfully, I am happy he is back. I feel I have a real friend near, and I never stop loving him. We've always had that spark and James knows when and when not to give me the boundaries that I hold so near and dear to my heart.

"So, you see, I'm just not ready for what you're wanting." I hesitated to say

James sat forward on the bench where we decided to sit and take in the view and took a long deep breath. "Look, Leah, All I've ever wanted to do since high school was to be with you. Now I understand what you've been thru, and it can be a lot to adjust to a whole new way of living. All I'm asking is the chance to continue to be in your life and whatever you need I'm here; I'll do it for you." He proclaimed.

I didn't know what to make of that. I know James can be a little pushy when it comes to getting his way but, I know he was in my corner. I touched James on his back and wrapped one arm around him placing my chin on his shoulder. "My heart says yes but I need more time is what my mental is telling me."

James already knows I've been thru a lot with Lewis and who could blame me for needing time to process all that I had gone thru. I guess you can say James was being a little selfish by only seeing what he wanted or what he thinks is best for me. That wouldn't make him any different than the piece of shit I just got rid of.

"I'm willing to do whatever it takes, if space is what you need then that's okay with me."

He moved back home on schedule. The anticipation of him being near has created butterflies in my stomach ever since I found out. I was at the shop completing some finishing touches on a client's hair when he walked in. He scanned the shop searching for me. Once he spotted me and our eyes connected, I knew right then that taking a chance with James was worth it. After not seeing him since my visit to New York has made my heart yearn to be close to him. Who knows what the future may hold? I have grown from my experiences in so many ways, I'm content with making mistakes or not doing anything at all.

There is one thing I won't do is deny myself and as I stand here awaiting the embrace from his arms, I won't deny that I'm in love with James more than the first day I fell.

Chapter 58 [JAMES]

"Hey, you!" I just landed and went straight from the airport to the salon that Leah works. I couldn't go another minute without seeing her. I walked in and spotted her and those big brown eyes. She was glowing. As I embraced her, I took in breaths of her essence that had an aroma that calmed my soul. I held her so long she had to remind me to let her breathe.

"Ok, James." She laughed. "I can't breathe." I began to kiss her neck. Leah wasn't about displaying much affection in public, but I didn't care. I loved to catch her off guard; it takes her out of her comfort zone. She had this adorable grin on her face as if she was trying to hold back how happy she was. There were a few onlookers and Leah is a discreet person so I toned it down a bit.

"Are you ready, I got us a cab waiting?" I was anxious to get to the apartment and start unpacking. Leah has been very helpful in assisting me in apartment hunting. My transition would probably have been a disaster if it wasn't for her.

"Yeah almost, let me get my bag." I stood there watching Leah grab stuff. I looked up and scoped the shop and not to my surprise Leah and I were center stage.

"How yall ladies doing?" I said with a little wave out of feeling awkward.

"HEY!" [they responded in unison]

Leah put her bag over her shoulder with a little chuckle. "Ok, I think that's our cue. Let's go, Casanova." She pushed me toward the door. The ladies laughed and teased until we were unable to hear the rambling of their opinions and ideas that didn't matter. I opened the cab door for Leah and got in after she did. "Yes, River Parkway please." The driver pulled off down the street and I looked over at Leah as she looked around at her surroundings outside of the window.

At this very moment, I knew this is where I wanted to be. I loved who I was when I was with Leah. We ended up at the apartment building, I paid the cab driver and gave a tip. The front desk had my key. "How you feel?" I asked Leah trying to distract myself from the excitement I felt of sharing this milestone with her.

"I'm good. I can't wait to see what you're going to do with your apartment." She said with a huge smile. "I'm proud of you." Her face just lit up with every word that she said.

We opened the door to the apartment, and it felt just like home. If felt as if a fresh clean slate was laid out right in front of us. It felt good and with Leah being here at that same moment put it all in perspective with me. She was meant to be a part of my life.

Chapter 59 [DENISE]

My painful battle with having my abortion was growing like weeds and I didn't know how to kill the pain that was destroying the field of love I wanted my heart to possess. I just could not forgive myself. I would often go out drinking or smoke a little hay on a bad day. My sexual escapades were nothing more than an activity to take my mind off the fear of being alone. I've watched my mother growing up and ever since my Dad her trust in men seem to completely vanish. I don't want to settle for that in my life. I must learn to love myself for love to love me.

I came back home to check on Mom. She's been doing well despite the cancer scare we had about a year ago. It was New Year's Eve and we were getting ready for watch service. We had a tradition every new year's holiday. We would go to watch the service then come back home and have breakfast. We've been doing this since I was a little girl.

"Mom, I'll have to run by the pharmacy to pick up something really quick before we head out to church, is that okay?" I know how prompt my mother would like to be but I'm driving so the old lady will have to sacrifice.

"That's fine dear, just done be too long."

"Yes ma'am, I'll be back." I closed the front door behind me and hopped in my rental car. I drove to the Eckerd pharmacy on the corner to pick up some feminine products. Mom didn't have anything that I could use. My body has started to get back to normal since the procedure, which is a good thing physically but spiritually, I'll need more work.

I walked toward the back of the store and to my surprise, I wasn't the only one in need of the feminine product section.

"Denise?"

"Nathan?"

I haven't seen or heard from Nathan in a long time. The last thing I heard is that he did do what he wanted and that was to go into culinary arts and that he had moved Houston. I wasn't sure what to say in this moment.

Nathan looked nervous. He started rustling with something in his hand and glanced at it. "so, what have you been up to?" he asked.

"Oh, the usual; work, some play." I laughed nervously. Talking to Nathan was like walking into the unknown. I had no idea who he was anymore. "You?"

"The same, and a probably a little bit of too much play." I looked down at his hand and realized why he was in the feminine section. He had a pregnancy test in his hand. Once he realized I blew his cover he took a deep sigh. "Yeah, she might be."

"Oh my God, Nathan." I put my hand over my chest. "Are you serious?"

"Yeah, I'm scared as hell but excited. I planned on asking her to marry me first but…" he made a gesture of things happen or we allow them to.

"Well, Congratulations!"

"Thanks. I appreciate that."

"So, who's the lucky lady, anybody we know?" I teased.

"I'm not sure, she did go to your high school. Does Marissa, Marissa Orville ring a bell?" he asked trying to see if he could jog my memory.

You damn right I know her. The odds of Marissa and Nathan being together would have not crossed my mind. The fact that he said her name sent me in my feelings. Who was she to deserve Nathan? Bad enough she stole James from Leah back in the day now Nathan. Don't get me wrong Nathan and I had broken up years ago, but we never had real closure. What am I talking about? This relationship was eight years ago when I was younger and dumber and didn't know what love was about. At times I still don't. "yeah, I think I recall see her around." I lied. I just wanted to get out of there. "Well, Nathan I have to go. Mom is…" I corrected myself. "My mom is waiting on me to take her to church." I started walking toward the register to avoid any more conversation with him.

"Oh, ok. Nice seeing you?" he stood there with a confused look on his face.

I waved and kept walking until I got inside the car. I sat there for a moment thinking about everyone that I knew growing up, was doing just that; growing. I felt I was in an emotional whirlwind. I'm not sure why hearing Nathans's news bothered me. I didn't know what I was doing in my life. I felt if I went to college and got a degree then I would be proud, I would feel accomplished and fulfilled. This was not so.

I started the car and began to drive back to my mothers' home. I thought about all the relationships I've had since leaving home. Coming from the humble beginnings of my life, being molested, no real father figure until later in life; sometimes I have a fear that these past demons will destroy me in the future if I let it. My eyes became open at a young age of how a man can have control over you. The mental damage of sexual abuse can be crippling and offsetting in the daily life of the victim. It has taken me years to learn how to cope and some people are not as lucky as me to have had help by a professional.

I honked the horn for Mom to come out. I watched her walk to the car and get in. I was curious about her thoughts of my past, why didn't she do anything. "Ready?" I helped her with her seat belt.

"Yeah, let's go. Let's leave the past in the past so we can start over toward the future." Mom said.

"You know what, mom. You're right. The past is the past." I grabbed my mother's hand and embraced it. Her face beamed as the sunlight passed over each time it was not blocked by the trees on the highway. "I'm glad I have the chance to start over again with you by my side. I love you mama."

"I love you more."

With love, anything is sustainable; even when tainted.

EPILOGUE

Nathan

"It's a boy!" the doctor said. I know that there is a quick moment of euphoria for the mother but the feeling that I am having now must be close to it. Seeing my son born out of the woman I'm madly in love with is the best thing that a man can ask God for. I had Marissa's hand and kissed it gently along with her forehead. She had to have a cesarean due to complications with her placenta.

As they took my son over to clean him, I noticed he didn't cry, and he looked quite blue. I looked over at Marissa and she looked out of it. She began to complain about being extremely cold and the nurses had warm blankets for her. I didn't like the way she looked, and she started shaking uncontrollably.

"Marissa?"

"I'm…. here, Nate. I'm just cold." She struggled to say. I looked over at our son again and more people had surrounded him. I told Marissa I would be right back. The anesthesiologist gave a nudge to me that it was okay.

By the time I went over there I saw my son take his first breath and he began to wail. My heart stopped the whole time until then. They wrapped him up and gave him to me to hold. I couldn't believe I was holding a life that was apart of me. How can I already love someone so much and would do anything for them before knowing them?

I walked back over to Marissa who had settled a little from shaking. I sat on the stool beside the table she was laid out on.

"Babe?" she turned her head and begin to smile once she realized I had our child in my arms.

"Let me see." I leaned a little toward Marissa so she may see his face. Her face took on another form that I had never seen before. She took on an angelic form as if she had seen the beginning and the end of life.

[BEEP]

"What's going on?" I asked the anesthesiologist.